Previous story........Before I Died....

Tilly had gone through a really traumatic tim
and mentally abused by a previous boyfriend. He had stalked her and eventually her fiance had been murdered.

He was a very dangerous man with a completely split personality. His head was two people

Tyler the normal part and *Simon* the dangerous, aggressive and totally mad part.

Tilly (or as *Simon* calls her Matilda) had gone through so much but is now settled and married to Toby, the policeman who managed to catch *Simon*.

Chapter EIGHTEEN - Before I died

The start of the week.

This week was going to be one big roller coaster for me I was sure. It was now Monday and on Saturday afternoon at 4.45pm I was going to fly to New Zealand travelling on my own. That alone was a big step for me as I had never flown alone before, let alone on such a long journey. Still, as my mother had pointed out to me, I was flying first class.

It was going to be a busy week as I had promised to go and see my gran in the nursing home and she had instructed me to "bring that lovely young man of yours with you," and had added "if only I was a few years younger....well quite a few"

We had been invited to dinner at my brothers on the Wednesday and my mum too. My mum had also insisted that we do a 'ladies that lunch' on

Tuesday, just her, me and Cassandra. "She'll find somebody to have the boys I'm sure", Mum had said.

I wanted to get a present for Toby's parents although he had said it wasn't necessary I still wanted to get them something. Mum, Cassie and I went into every shop in Guildford looking for something suitable but drew blank after blank until Cassie suddenly said "Why not just a picture of you guys on your wedding day but in a silver fame that is inscribed. Really boring I know but it is very personal and shows you have put some thought into it."

"Well it shows you put some thought into it" I laughed but it is a great idea. So we found a nice frame and went off of lunch while they engraved it for me.

We had a wonderful evening on Wednesday with mum, Cassie and Tom, and of course the boys, who won't let a visit from anybody go by without being totally involved, or a part of it anyway. Cassie cooked us a fantastic meal and after picking away on cheese for what seemed forever we drank glass after glass of port. It was a good job we were all staying over. I sat there and looked at my family, my beloved family, and thought just how very lucky I was.

The thought of the upcoming trial was in the back of our thoughts but none of us said a word about it, there was no way we were going to ruin this wonderful evening.

I was lucky that I didn't have to be called as a witness in the trial as I had already given so many statements and had video answered several questions from the defence lawyer. They had given me and Simon's other victims this choice because he intended to plead guilty. They said we had suffered enough and would not need to be in court where we would be looking at him. For this we were all grateful. I did wonder why he had so easily agreed to plead guilty. Did he think it would be in his favour? I had no idea but was very glad anyway. They did say though that if there was any change in his plea we might be called, in which case Toby had said it could be adjourned until I could return from New Zealand. So I was going.....regardless of anything.

Friday night Toby took me for a curry. Not particularly romantic I know but as it is my favourite meal of all time he knew it would make me happy. We walked to the Indian and had a great meal with lots of wine. Then, in our drunken state, as soon as we got home, made fantastic love at least twice or maybe three times (Toby would say three anyway) that night.

Morning arrived all too soon and with rather heavy heads we showered and dragged ourselves down to the kitchen. Luckily I had had the forethought to pack the day before. God knows what I would have packed if I had left it till this morning.

Beside my coffee cup was a box, about the size of a packet of cigarettes, wrapped in beautiful gold wrapping paper and embellished with a huge gold bow. Toby was grinning at me.

"Go on then, open it" he said. It was a beautiful gold charm bracelet. There were two charms on it, one was a heart about the size of the head of a drawing pin and the other, two tiny joined together figurines, a bride and groom. "Us" he said proudly, "Forever" .

I did cry then, not with sadness of going away from him but with so much love for him. He fixed the bracelet on my wrist and kissed my hand. "Have a wonderful time darling, and I will be with you there very very soon, Oh and of course - miss me!"

My taxi arrived early afternoon leaving me plenty of time just in case of traffic and also so I could have a wonder around the duty frees before my flight to maybe get some perfume etc.. I had decided to take a cab as I hate long drawn out goodbyes so thought it would be easier. Anyway Toby was supposed to be at work really. We kissed a long lingering kiss at the door of the taxi, the driver was looking the other way for a bit but then turned and said "Aw common guys, I do have other fares to collect today" one more quick peck and I was in the cab and on my way to the airport.

As I was travelling first class I was treated like royalty. I was shown into this posh lounge where there was anything I wanted to drink and lots of stuff to eat. Not that I wanted to eat anything, but I don't know if it was because I was nervous or excited - I did manage to sink three large gin and tonics before I boarded.

I was towards the front of the first class area and next to me was a lovely chatty American lady who told me her name was Nancy.

"First flight ?" she asked just as we were taking off. "It's just I saw you holding on tightly to the arm rests as we took off, don't worry sweetheart it's going to be a blast. I travel about twenty times a year, have done for donkeys years and nothing has ever happened to me yet".

She was a bit of a life saver really as I was a little nervous. The flight attendants started the safety video which Nancy totally ignored of course, well, she said she flew twenty times a year so what did she have to learn about safety. She could probably tell them a thing or two. She prattled on and on but I was only half listening. Then the bit about switching off all phones and electrical devices etc. came on and I remembered I hadn't turned off my phone. I took it out of my bag quickly and switched it off, thinking I would put in on flight safe mode and switch it back on later.

What I had no idea about at that moment was that there had been a collision back in London in the early hours of that day involving a police prison transporter and a bus. Apparently (and totally unknown to me) the prison transporter was carrying three prisoners who were due to appear in court. One of them was Simon. One of the others was the boss of a massive drug ring. The bus episode was obviously a fix. Three security guards had ended up in hospital. One had been killed and the three prisoners had escaped. Simon was free !!!!! And I had no idea.

I soon settled in my seat and put a movie on the small screen in front of me. It had been a while since I had been on a plane and then only on short flights to Spain and France. I had never seen the options available on the latest planes. Wow, I thought ,I can watch movies that haven't even been released yet. I chose one featuring Brad Pitt...what else...for two reasons. Firstly because it was a novelty and secondly Nancy would see I was engrossed in it and perhaps stop talking for a little while. She was a lovely woman but boy could she talk. She had a real southern American accent which sounded nice for a short time but a little grating after a couple of hours.

As it was such a long journey there was going to be a stop off at Dubai for three hours. This turned out to be a real treat. Nancy, although still very chatty, was a perfect travelling companion after all. We went into the airport lounge and she both entertained and thrilled me with all her stories of her travels. She had a book publishing company and travelled all over the world meeting authors and outlets, book signings and lots and lots of parties. She had met so many people I suggested she write her autobiography. "That my darling will happen one day and when it does and you read it you had better hold on to your hat".

The three hour stop over went in an instant with Nancy at the helm of our entertainment. And all too soon we were called back to continue our journey. I thanked Nancy for making my trip, so far anyway, so very memorable.

Back on our flight I fiddled again to find another film to watch but ended up watching the entire first series of Downton Abbey, one of my favourite TV dramas. Nancy was snoozing beside me making soft snoring noises which made me smile to myself.

A couple of hours into the second leg we were offered drinks and a little later more drinks and then a really nice dinner. I didn't know that they served such luxury on planes. We had proper cutlery and plates and everything. On the short flights I had experienced it was coffee in a paper cup or miniature spirit and tiny mixer can and a plastic glass hardly big enough for either. The movie was good and then I tuned into a topical London magazine show. I was only half watching as I was beginning to feel a little drowsy until a ticker tape or current news began to appear across the bottom of the screen. At first I thought I was seeing things but as I watched it again and again it began to dawn on me that it was current and true. It said there had been a crash in the city in the early hours of today and that three prisoners escaped. Then it went on to name them. My drowsiness disappeared instantly as I watched in wonder at the tape. Nancy leaned across and asked why I had suddenly started to whimper under my breath and to see just what was I looking at.

"Wow those are great dogs, do you have a dog at home?" I realised she was actually watching the magazine program and they had six or seven types of huge long haired dogs. "I wouldn't want to have to groom one of them eh!" she said "I have a little Poodle myself, they don't moult you know. Oh I do miss him when I travel, still Bernie my husband looks after him while I'm away, he loves him almost as much as I do" I had switched off from her conversation and I think she realised as she leaned back into her own seat and started fiddling with her monitor.

I was in shock, why hadn't Toby got in touch and told me what had happened, then I realised I hadn't switched my phone back on. Just at that moment the flight attendant asked if we wanted anything more to drink The state I was in I would have drunk her bar dry but I just asked for a bottle of wine. Nancy gave me a strange look as if to say, what the hell, she then smiled a great big smile and she too asked for a bottle of wine. I have no idea just what the flight attendant thought but she obliged without comment, just a smile and a "certainly madam". I poured the first glass out and tried to get my head around what had happened. I was tempted to turn on my phone to see if I had received a text from Toby but I stopped short of doing it, deciding that I probably didn't really want to know just what was going on in London. I'm sure they would catch him soon enough. That was a rubbish thought, he was incredible at disappearing.

A second glass of wine, then a third........

I feel like I'm floating, yes I am floating, up and down, twisting like a kite. I am feeling like a feather, yes that's it, a beautiful white feather dancing in the breeze, I feel happy, content. More content than I have ever felt before, a strange feeling like I haven't a care in the whole wide world, arrrh floating, floating I feel free, I feel wonderful, I feel....what is that noise that has broken into my beautiful silent world, a loud noise, a harsh noise. I can't quite fathom what it is but it's getting louder and louder. I still have no idea but still it gets louder, louder, louder....it's screaming, I can hear screaming, I can hear so much screaming and shouting, I can hear people shouting then more screaming more screaming more screaming !!!!!

I am dead, I realise that now, and the screaming I heard was all the other people dying around me as the plane plummeted in to the ocean. I don't know quite how I feel other than very very sad. Sad that I will miss all the things I was hoping for in my new life. Arrrh my new life, I have waited for a long long time to get my new life and now it was ready to collect me. I will miss it. The train that was to take me to my future has just left the station without me....no more looking forward, no more plans. I am dead !

"Tilly, Tilly", a genteel nudging suddenly is coming into my thoughts, what is going on, I am dead who is nudging me and how come I can feel it. I am dead...."Tilly Tilly are you alright" that voice again, that nudging. I am suddenly back in my seat in the plane. It is Nancy nudging me, she is leaning over me and her face is looking very concerned "Are you alright

Tilly, you were screaming in your sleep, nearly woke all the other passengers up, did you have a bad dream dear?"

I'm not dead, I realise that now, it must all have been a terrible dream. My god I'm alive, I'm alive. I almost want to kiss Nancy with the relief of it. "Too much wine deary" she is saying "you drank nearly a whole bottle, no wonder you had a bad dream."

The relief I feel is unbelievable. That dream was so real, but I'm alive.

"We'll be there soon" Nancy is saying. They'll be bringing us breakfast in an hour or so. Shall I call them and get them to bring you some coffee now?"

"No It's OK" I say "I'll wait for the breakfast to come.

I am day dreaming, I really thought I was dead. Was it a dream, I turn to see Nancy with a mirror in one hand and a lipstick in the other. Surely if I am dead this wouldn't be happening. "Nancy" I say and she turns to face me "Tell me I am not in a dream"

"You are definitely not in a dream" she is telling me "Was it a bad one then ? That dream you just had?"

I don't know quite how to answer that as I am still not entirely sure this is real. Was it a dream? It was so very vivid, am I alive or is this what it's like when you are dead ?

"I know this is a funny question" I say "but can you tell me what day it is?"

Nancy is looking very puzzled "It's Sunday morning, remember we got on the plane on Saturday afternoon the 15th and now it is Sunday morning the 16th, arr sweetie are you getting a bit confused with the time differences?

To say relief is washing over me is an understatement. So it was all a dream. I am alive, I am well, I am in a plane going to New Zealand to stay with my brand new in-laws and soon my darling new husband will be joining me.

"Are you feeling better now sweetheart" I hear Nancy saying "you are still very white"

"I'm fine now thank you" I say "and do you know I am ready for some breakfast now. I'm starving!"

"Well I think it is on it's way" she says "I can smell bacon."

Breakfast has arrived and I am tucking into mine as if I had never eaten before. After all, I have a life, I am alive and things are good. They have just cleared everything away and are now serving a second round of coffees. "Shall we pop a little brandy in ours?" Nancy has just asked. Now I know it is early but what the hell, "Yes why not" Nancy has just summoned an attendant to bring us a small brandy each.

Here you are madam, I hear , a voice that sounds a bit familiar, I am turning my head to say thank you, "Here you go MATILDA" !!!!!!!...

BANG..

THE END

Prologue -- After I died !!!!

"Oh my god my head, my head!" Tilly shouted and tried to pull herself up into a sitting position.

Her head rocked and felt as if a huge boulder was inside banging its way to get out through her skull. Toby suddenly appeared in her room.

"Steady there darling" he spoke almost too quietly for Tilly to understand him. He placed a cool damp cloth onto her forehead and tried to lay her back down onto the bed. Tilly's eyes were wide and wild looking as she fought him with all the power she could muster.

Then suddenly she just went limp and flopped back against the pillows, closing her eyes and very softly saying "No! please NO! please NO!"

CHAPTER 1

New Zealand

(18 months after their wedding)

"Excuse me" A voice suddenly broke into Toby's thoughts as he sat with Tilly, just watching as her chest slowly rose up and down. He wasn't sure why he had to sit and watch as he was sure she wasn't going to stop breathing but he felt compelled to keep a check anyway. "Excuse me" the voice said again, "I am sorry to disturb you but Doctor Rolf wondered, if you have a moment before you leave, if you could pop by his office?"

Toby lifted his head to see the pretty nurse Tompak standing in the doorway looking a little flushed, almost as if she felt she had invaded a private moment and was embarrassed to do so. Toby gave her one of his friendly smiles to put her mind at rest and agreed he would go along to the doctor's office in a few minutes. Nurse Tompak, or Suzie, as Toby had got used to calling her, *after all when your wife is in somebody's care for a long time first name terms seem to be the norm,* Suzie smiled back, her heart melting, she had fallen for Toby at their very first meeting but in such tragic circumstances it was totally unprofessional and inappropriate as he was so obviously in love with his wife, but it didn't stop her dreaming of meeting somebody who could make her feel as she did every time she set eyes on him.

Toby leaned over and kissed his wife although she was in a deep sleep and wouldn't know if he was there or not but it made him feel better for the physical contact.

Leaving her room he took one last look before pulling the door to behind him. He walked down the corridor to Doctor Rolf's office and knocked softly on the door.

"Come in" a voice from within commanded his entry so Toby twisted the knob and gently pushed the door open and entered a rather elegant looking office. The doctor had his head down over some paperwork on his desk but moved it slightly up motioning Toby to sit in the chair opposite him. "I won't keep you a moment" he said pleasantly "I just have to finish this while it is fresh in my mind".

Toby sat as directed and waited for the doctor to finish whatever it was he was working on. His eyes wandered around the room. Not like a doctor's office at all, he was thinking. Nice expensive looking furniture adorned the whole room; pictures on the walls, some reproductions of well known original paintings were on two walls. Another wall was almost covered by a huge dresser, made of beautiful natural coloured woods blended together. It was an amazing piece and Toby had trouble taking his eyes off it, there were shelves decorated with silver framed pictures of whom Toby supposed were members of the doctor's family. Several children at various stages of growing up and a very, not beautiful but would probably be described as handsome woman, presumably Mrs Rolf. A gentle cough suddenly broke into Toby's thoughts making him feel guilty for staring but the doctor had looked up and was ready to speak.

"I expect you are wondering why I asked you to come and see me?" He didn't wait for a response just continued "I am sorry that Tilly hasn't made as much of an improvement as I was initially hoping and I am even more sorry to have to tell you that I think the time has come for her to be moved to a more specialised institution." Toby started to interrupt but the doctor lifted a hand to halt him "let me finish please" he said. "The thing is Toby, Tilly has had a complete mental shut down, she was so traumatised by all that happened. When she got together with you she was so happy and pushed all the traumas to the back of her brain. But then it forced itself forward in a rush when she was on the plane heading over here and bang! She has now shut down completely. I thought at first sedation and plenty of rest could bring her back but she is not improving quickly enough, in fact she hasn't improved at all and I am worried that she might never recover."

At this statement Toby made a small noise in his throat and tears began to appear in the corners of his eyes. He didn't try to speak but just looked at the doctor.

Doctor Rolf continued "Please, I am not asking you to give up on her, there is still a small chance that she may make a full or at least partial recovery but it won't be here. She will need a specialist in mental trauma to monitor her and work out just what to do next and I am afraid that is not my area of expertise. I could tell you to keep her here and we could carry on letting her rest but it has been over a year now with little or no improvement, so for your sake as much as hers she will need to go to Harwood Place where they will know just how to proceed. I am so sorry"

CHAPTER 2

CHERTSEY – ENGLAND

Helen was standing in front of the wardrobe mirror staring at the reflection of the girl looking back at her when suddenly, from behind, a gruesome face appeared making her almost jump out of her skin.

"What the hell?" she screamed, jumping to one side only to see her friend Ashling laughing hysterically and peeling the rubber Halloween mask from her face. "I nearly had a heart attack you mad cow!" Helen squealed but was laughing almost as much as her friend. "Where the bloody hell did you get that gross thing ?" she said, picking up the mask and examining it. "It's bloody horrible!"

"I've had it for years" Ashling replied "but I only found it in the bottom of my cupboard the other day and have been dying for a moment to use it..."

"And now you have, you bitch!" Helen replied "You had better lock it away or I might just be trying it out on you when you least expect it!" they both laughed as Ash sprawled out on Helen's bed, picked at a lose thread, wound it around her fingers until it came away and then discretely squashed it back into the fabric.

"Right come on now, who are you trying to impress in that outfit then? Got a hot date, my friend?"

"Yes actually I have and I am already late, so help me out Ash and tell me if this looks OK"

Ashling looked her up and down with a mock frown on her face "Hmmmm" she said " not too bad for an ugly old bag like you, I think you may just be passable" and saying that she got up from the bed and waltzed out of the room, returning seconds later with her almost new leather jacket over her arm. "Here you go" she said " this will finish it off a treat." Helen started to protest as she knew it was her friend's pride and joy, but Ashing shushed her and just said "Call it my way of getting you laid, after all it has been some time eh?" and they both burst out laughing again, which was a frequent occurrence between the friends.

Friends since school they had always had the dream that once they were "grown up" they would get a flat together and have a great time just having fun. Well they got the flat and they did have a lot of fun for the first two years or so but Ashling now had a serious boyfriend and Helen felt a little bit in the way at times. She was, of course, really happy for her friend and she thought Jamie was a great guy but she was just a tad sad that their friendship was not, obviously, quite as it used to be.

To begin with Ashling tried to include Helen in as many activities and outings as she could and they all went around together as a threesome. They had great nights at the local pub quizzes; they went to loads of films and the odd party or two. Jamie had often brought a friend along to make up a foursome with a vague hope that Helen might fall for one of them but it never happened. They never gave Helen the impression she was in the way, of course, but it soon became apparent that Jamie and Ashling were going along the serious route and so Helen pulled back somewhat and started to mix in her own single circle.

It was at one of these get-togethers a week ago that Tyler had suddenly appeared on the scene. Helen was sitting alone waiting for the others to show up when he walked into the pub with a bunch of guys just about to embark on a mad stag night. Helen spotted him immediately he walked into the pub. He was really good looking and stood out from the rest of them as he seemed sober and not in such quite high spirits. The crowd had all headed to the bar but Tyler had spotted Helen and headed towards her.

"I couldn't help but notice your glass is empty" his opening line, not too corny she had thought, well a bit but hey he is really good looking. Within the hour Helen had parted company with her friends and Tyler his stag buddies who had moved on to their next venue, the pub next door. He explained to Helen that he hadn't really wanted to go out with them but just felt he should, although he knew the guy getting married, he didn't really know many of the others.

By this time he had found out her name, where she worked, favourite film etc., she in turn had found out his name was Tyler but nothing more. They had another drink together and then he said he thought he should catch up with the stag party.

Helen was relaying this story to Ashling as she applied a little more eye makeup and sipped at the glass of wine Ashling had brought in for her.

"So" Ashling was asking "you are meeting him again now?"

"Well" Helen continued "When he said he was heading off I started to walk back next door to where my friends were and was thinking to myself, well that was a waste of time, when he suddenly appeared beside me and touched my arm. He asked if I would like to go out for a drink sometime, well that sometime is now. So bloody well check me over to see if I look OK or I'll be late!" and with that she laughed and threw one of her cuddly toys at Ashling, put on the special jacket and did a little dah-dah!

After she had been assured by her friend that she looked a million dollars Helen eventually left the little flat and started to walk very fast to the main road to try and grab a cab. She only had a mile or so to go and would have walked it under normal circumstances but she was running a little late and it had started to drizzle. On her third attempt she managed to get a cab to stop but half way there they were stuck in a bit of traffic. By the time she arrived at the pub she was more than half an hour late. Tyler wasn't in the pub but when Helen looked outside she saw he was walking down the road away from it. She stood for a moment trying to decide whether to call after him or just say fuck it but calling after him won and she shouted as loud as she could. "Tyler!". He turned around but instead of a smile on his face he looked like he was going to murder somebody. Then as quickly as it appeared it disappeared and he did smile.

"I'm sorry I'm late" Helen cooed, "it was the traffic." Tyler shushed her,

"Don't worry about it Helen, it was just that I thought you weren't going to show up, I hate lateness, it always makes me think that I have been stood up, stupid I know but it is just one of those idiot things that has stuck with me since childhood"

"Well I am here now so how about we go get that drink you promised me" Helen said and linking arms with him started to walk back towards the pub thinking to herself that he must have had an event in his life to prompt such feelings of insecurity.

They only stayed in the pub for a short time as Tyler said he was starving and fancied a curry. Helen was not a curry fan and was in no way hungry but didn't want to spoil the evening so agreed. Tyler ate a starter then a huge spicy vindaloo curry and even finished off the remains of the korma Helen had hardly touched.

"Not a fan of curry then?" Tyler had remarked stuffing naan bread into his already full mouth and spitting little globules of curry all over the white table cloth, which Helen found very unattractive. Once the meal was done and the bill was presented Helen watched as Tyler pulled out his wallet only to see it was empty.

"I had a fifty pound note in here earlier, some bastard must have swiped it, sorry Helen this one will have to be on you." He quickly put his wallet away and Helen went to get her purse out then thought to herself, hang on a minute, I bought the drinks in the pub so he hasn't even had his wallet out tonight for somebody to steal his money, and also he had a banker's card in full view, so why didn't he use that? But instead of pointing this out to him she just got her card out and paid, thinking this is the first and last date with you mate.

They walked to the taxi rank and Helen was surprised when Tyler jumped in behind her.

"I thought we could share Helen, that's OK isn't it?" The cab took Tyler home first as it was the opposite direction to the rank and as Tyler said it would be better for the driver to take him first. Helen didn't understand any of that argument but went along with it as she was beginning to think maybe Tyler was a bit of a nut and she didn't want to upset him just in case he turned nasty. Once they got to his street, or where he said he lived anyway, he announced that he would get out at the end of the road, "No need to go right down it" he had said. Jumping out he blew Helen a kiss and said

"You can sort out the dosh eh honey, you know I've had my money half inched, I owe you babe, I'll call you!" and with that he was gone and Helen was more than a bit relieved.

Once back at her flat she crept in quietly just in case Ashling was either at it with Jamie or had gone for an early night, neither of which turned out to be right. Ashling was sitting on the sofa with her legs tucked under her munching on the remains of a left over pizza.

"What happened to you?" she said as Helen crept in with a face like thunder "Not a good date eh"? Helen threw herself down on another of the chairs and dropped her bag on the floor, then spying a half finished bottle of wine and a glass, even though it had been used, poured some of the red liquid into it and took a huge glug. Ashling just sat and waited, she knew Helen would need a few minutes to calm down after whatever was bothering her. She was patient, she had news of her own to talk to Helen about but thought it could keep for a few minutes longer anyway. After the third swallow of wine Helen relaxed, slipped off Ashling's jacket and her shoes and she too tucked her legs underneath her ready to tell her friend all about her awful date.

"Well", Ashling said after Helen had explained the evening to her " It sounds like you had a lucky escape, looks like he was just after a free evening, you're not contemplating seeing him again if he calls are you ?" Helen looked thoughtful for a moment just to wind her friend up...then as Ashling sat open mouthed ready to berate her she burst out laughing.

"Of course not you idiot, what do you take me for?" she said " For one thing I don't think I could afford to date him on my salary" at this they both laughed together. "Now", Helen continued, tell me about your evening"

Ashling lifted the wine bottle and slowly poured herself half a glass, then offered it to Helen who took it and topped up her own. Helen could see tears starting to appear in Ashling's eyes and realised immediately that something had gone wrong with her friend's night.

"Come on Ash, tell me all about it, did you and Jamie have a row or something?" She moved over to the sofa and squashed next to her friend.

"He is going abroad to work Helen" Ashling said "He'll be gone for six whole months" She then proceeded to tell her friend all about Jamie's job with the construction company he had been working for since he left Uni and how they have a new project beginning in the United Arab Emirates. "Six whole months though Helen" she said "How am I going to last without him for six whole months?" Then the long awaited tears started to flow.

Helen put her arm around her and let her sob for a few minutes.

"Now come on Ash" she said "I thought you two were planning to get hitched next year, well isn't that why he is doing this, to get some tax free money behind him so you can start to plan for the future?"

"Huh" Ashling replied "You must have been talking to him 'cos that is exactly what he said, but I can't bear to be without him for all that time, just suppose....yes just suppose" she almost shouted as Helen tried to interrupt, "he meets somebody else while he's there, suppose she is beautiful and tanned and slim and......."

At this point Helen put a gentle hand over Ash's mouth and, looking straight into her eyes said, "Listen, stupid!, Jamie loves you, you know he does, he's only doing this to make a better life for the two of you, honestly Ash just trust him. He is a lovely guy and I am sure there is no chance he is going to want to meet anybody else, anyway he will be too busy working".

Ashling started to calm down, listening to her friends kind words, contemplating whether she believed them or not.

"I suppose you might be right" she said "he did actually say that the company would pay half of the fare for me to go out and visit him at least three times during the six months so I suppose maybe it won't be all bad!" at this moment the phone rang and Ashling grabbed at it.

"I'm sorry too", Helen heard her saying as she took the phone into the bedroom and shut the door behind her.

The next morning Helen found Ashling in the tiny kitchen singing. She settled herself at the tiny table and accepted the mug of coffee Ashling handed her.

"Well, what was said then, I know it wasn't a row or anything as I could hear you laughing and making kissy noises down the phone" Helen said grinning.

"Oh Helen it's all going to be fine. He said he is going to get me an engagement ring before he goes and we are going to have a great party and then, also before he goes, he is going to book me at least two flights to go and stay with him. On top of all that he said we can go shopping while I am there and I can buy my wedding dress, apparently there are loads of designer shops over there, although he said he won't want to see what I buy! Oh Helen I love him so very much!"

Helen stood up and threw her arms around her friend with genuine love

"Oh and of course you must be my bridesmaid Helen, hey, here's an idea, maybe we could both go to Dubai together on one of my trips and we could get you a bridesmaid dress". Suddenly it was like a teenage sleep over in their kitchen. Both girls making plans and getting each other excited. Luckily it was a Saturday and as neither of them had anything planned for the morning so they made toast, scrambled some eggs and topped up on their coffee mugs then settled to enjoy the planning of the wedding and the visits to Dubai.

Later that day Jamie came to pick Ashling up for a trip to the pictures leaving Helen alone in the flat going through all brides magazines that they had both been looking through most of the afternoon. Ashling had ventured out to the local shop and bought what seemed like all they had in their stock!!

"Oh my god", Jamie had said laughing as he had walked in to find the two of them on the floor in the lounge with all the magazines around them and a giant note pad with what looked like a load of lists!! "I'm a dead man........or rather a very broke man "!!!

Helen had jumped up and thrown her arms around him planting a big kiss in his left cheek, "Congratulations mate" she said as he planted one back on hers and gently let her go,

"I can see I am going to have to keep a tight string on you two for the wedding, honestly a quick register office is all I really wanted...then adding quickly when he saw Ashling's face drop ......joking Ash of course you can have whatever you like, just let me keep a little of my hard earned cash for the honeymoon eh!"

After they had gone and Helen had settled with a glass of wine and the magazines, her mobile rang.

"Hi Helen".....at first Helen didn't recognise the voice but a nanosecond later realised who it was.

"Oh hi Tyler" she said, thinking to herself what the hell!!!!

"I was just wondering if you fancied coming out again tonight" he was asking.

Helen could hardly believe her ears and for a moment was a stuck for words but then re-organising her brain politely refused, saying she had already made plans. Tyler sounded a bit put out but persevered and requested they meet following Saturday instead. Helen was surprised as she thought he would have just taken the hint and so got a bit flustered and ended up agreeing to meet him. Before she had a chance to say where they should meet he was saying he would come around to her house and bring Pizza. Oh well she thought to herself, at least it would be a free dinner, and she had after all paid for the curry the other night, and of course he was rather hot even if he was tight !!

When Ashling came home Helen told her about the call.

"You're barking!" her friend said "Not only agreeing to see him again but letting him know where you live! You know Jamie and I are off that weekend, so I won't be around to give him the push out if you don't like him!" she continued laughing. "I think you should arrange to meet somewhere else"

Helen thought for a moment then said "I suppose you are right but I have already given him our address and he is bringing pizza, maybe I'll see him just this once, eat my money's worth of pizza then show him the door eh" she smiled "After all he does owe me doesn't he and he wasn't all that bad"

Ashling just shrugged and waltzed off into the kitchen shouting behind her as she went

"Well don't come crying to me if he starts stalking you every time he wants a curry paid for"

The week flew by and on the Friday night, as Ashling was packing her overnight bag ready for her weekend away the next day, Helen wandered into her bedroom.

"Have a great time at Jamie's sister's" she said" then continued "I've thought about Tyler coming round and thought that maybe after we have eaten our pizza I will suggest we go to the pub on the corner for a beer"

"Which you will make HIM pay for" Ashling interrupted and they both laughed.

It was Saturday so Helen did her usual stay in bed until ten o'clock habit. By the time she was up and dressed Ashling was well gone but had left a note in the kitchen worktop wishing Helen all the luck with her "date" and saying not to forget what they had discussed, and finishing with "I probably won't be home until later on Monday but I shall need to know all about your weekend, nudge, nudge, ha ha ha"

Idiot, Helen thought to herself, although touched that her friend had cared enough to leave a note. She put the note on the side by the kettle she had just turned on for her wake up coffee and made herself some toast. The day was going to drag for her without her friend there to banter with. Their usual Saturday ritual was to get up late, eat scrambled eggs or sometimes Helen would pop along to the patisserie for a pastry or two! Then they would usually hit the shops in the afternoon invariably ending up with some item of clothing that they didn't intend to buy but happened to be a "good bargain" Now, alone, she had just settled for two slices of toast drizzled with honey, mug of coffee and some old rubbish that happened to be on the TV.

Tyler had said he would come around with the Pizza at about 7.00pm so when it got to 7.20pm and he hadn't turned up Helen had decided he wasn't going to show, and although was relieved in a way was still annoyed that he would stand her up after the way he had behaved when she had showed up a bit late for their first date. By the time it got to eight O'clock she decided she wouldn't wait any longer so she donned her coat and headed for the pub. If he couldn't be bothered to show up at least she wasn't going to sit in on her own all night, her friends would be at the pub.

It was gone eleven when Helen began the walk back to her flat, a little worse for wear after the several gin and tonics her friends had bought her when she had told them she had been stood up. She had really enjoyed her evening but remembered half way home that she hadn't eaten so she stopped in the chippy for a bag of chips. By the time she was back at her flat she was feeling quite wobbly and was missing her mouth with each alternate chip, this started her giggling so much that she had trouble getting her key into the lock on her flat door. Just as she managed to get the door open a shadow appeared beside her.

"I was wondering just when you were going to show up" a snarly voice loomed out at her through the shadow, turning she saw Tyler staring at her with cold evil looking eyes "just where the fuck have you been all evening? Eh? Eh?" he said really nastily "You were supposed to be meeting me here tonight remember, you cow?"

Helen sobered within seconds and couldn't believe just what she was hearing

“Now look here for just one minute you shite” she said “I waited until eight o’clock for you to come with your bloody pizza! And anyway why am I answering to you, piss off and don’t come near me again!” And with that she started to go into her flat. She had only gone two steps when a violent crack to the back of her head sent her sprawling face down onto the floor.

CHAPTER 3

Ashling slipped out of the kitchen where Jamie and his sister were reminiscing about their mad childhood,

“I’m just going to pop to the shop on the corner to get a bottle of wine for tonight” she called over her shoulder although she wasn’t sure if either of them actually heard her.

She was in fact a little bored with all the “do you remember this and do you remember that” conversations that had been going on almost as soon as they both got up that morning. It was the same every time they visited each other. Much as she loved them they were very close and she did feel a little left out on occasions. Still, she thought, I suppose Helen and I bore the pants off Jamie a lot of the time with all our chatter and as they had both realised he was going to be away for a while she couldn’t really blame them that much. Anyway Cara’s husband Tony would be home from work soon so she would be able to chat to him. It was a shame he had had to go into work on that Sunday due to a computer problem at the office or else they would have gone out to lunch at the local pub. Anyway never mind she thought, I’ll go to the shop and while I’m out I’ll give Helen a call to see how her weird bloke was on their date!

She let the phone ring for what seemed like an awfully long minute and was just about to hang up when a man’s voice answered.

“Yes?” was all he said.

Ashling was a bit taken aback for a second, thinking she must have misdialled, but then realised that she had just short coded her friend so it had to be Helen’s phone,

"Oh is Helen there please?" she asked the strange voice immediately thinking to herself, dirty bitch, she's let him stay the night...wait till I see her. She was smiling at this thought when the voice broke in,

"Helen no longer wants to talk to you, in fact Helen wants you to collect your stuff from the flat tomorrow and not come around again. She will pack it up for you and leave it on the front door step".

"What the hell...arrh OK Helen, joke's over, I am sorry I left without waking you but I did leave you a note" she said fully expecting Helen to be killing herself laughing on the other end of the phone now.

Instead of that, the voice just said "This is no joke, we want you out" and with that the phone was disconnected.

Ashling tapped the short code again but it just rang and rang.

Not quite understanding what was going on Ashling bought her wine and headed back to Cara's house. Cara and Jamie had moved to the lounge by the time she got back with Cara curled up on the sofa watching some old film on the TV and Jamie reading the Sunday paper.

"I'm sorry if we get a bit carried away with our stories" she said as soon as Ashling walked in to the room, "You must have been bored silly but I promise we will stop now, well for a while anyway, can I get you a coffee and a piece of cake?"

"Yes I'd like some cake too please sis" Jamie peered from behind the newspaper, then turning to look at Ashling "Did you get some wine sweetheart"?

Ashling lifted two bottles high so Jamie could see them and thought to herself, so they did hear me, maybe I am not so invisible. "I got one red and one white is that OK?"

"Perfect, thanks Ash" Cara said getting up and taking the bottles out of Ashling's hands, "now you sit down and I'll get you your coffee and cake".

"Before you do" Ashling started "can you guys just listen a minute. I have just had a really strange conversation" She proceeded to tell them about the phone call to Helen.

Jamie just laughed, "She's having you on you twit" he said "You know what Helen is like, I bet she got on really well with that guy and he ended up staying and then thought it would be a great laugh to pretend she was mad with you. Remember when she was cross with you about forgetting to turn off the oven when her casserole got all dried up, she hid all your food under her bed so you had nothing to eat and then went out for the night, remember how she thought that was so very funny? Come on Ash you know she has a weird sense of humour, I'm sure when we get back tomorrow she will be laughing her socks off!"

Ashling smiled and agreed that maybe he was right but there was a little niggle inside her head that wouldn't settle, she had never known Helen to be nasty with her jokes and the guy she had spoken to sure was nasty. Still Jamie was the sensible one and he was convinced it was a joke so she was not going to let it spoil the rest of their stay with Cara and Tony. Tony had walked in just as they were discussing the phone call. He gave Ashling a hug and said that he had only caught the end of the conversation but it sounded to him like Jamie was right and they would all have a laugh about it when they got back. At this Cara said they should all forget about it and go into the kitchen where she had coffee and cake ready.

They had a great evening and after a few glasses of wine the telephone call was completely forgotten. Out came various games and at one point Cara had to rush to the loo before she "pee'd her pants" due to laughing so much at Ashling's attempt at playing an Ed Sheran song on the kazoo, the night was a blast. Helen totally forgotten.

Monday morning arrived and Jamie and Ashling were getting ready to go when Ashling's phone rang. She saw on the screen that is was Helen and a huge relief washed over her, she grabbed it and was just about to say OK you got me you cow, I almost believed your call yesterday, but before she could say more than “OK you”..... the nasty male voice cut in.

“Just to let you know your belongings have been left outside the door and I suggest you collect them soon before they get stolen. Oh and by the way the locks have now been changed this morning so don’t try and get in...you won’t” then he hung up.

Jamie was just coming down the stairs with their overnight bag but stopped as soon as he saw the look on Ashling's face

“What ever is the problem Ash?”, his concern was really genuine as the look on his now fiancé’s face was one he had never seen before. “Who was on the phone?” He could see that Ashling had her **p**hone still in her hand and was just staring at it.

“That was that bloke on Helen’s phone again” she started then burst into tears, “What a cow” she said “Jamie, he said they have changed the locks and put all my stuff outside the flat, why would she do something like that to me, I really don’t think it was a joke, or that call last night, I do think this whole thing is real!”

“Had you had any sort of a row or anything Ash ?” he was still thinking to himself that this must be some sort of sick joke.

“NO!” Ashling almost shouted at him. “We were fine when I came away, I did leave before she got up but I left a note, no we were fine, really, she has never been this horrible to me before, it just isn’t in her nature. Jamie I think something is very wrong, we need to get back there as soon as possible, please come on we must go now!”

Jamie could see how upset she was so put up no argument. He went into the kitchen where Cara was busy making toast and brewing coffee.

“Sorry Cara we have to go now” Jamie said. Cara looked hurt but saw the serious look on Jamie’s face and the tears in Ashling's eyes as she followed him into the room. She immediately thought they must have had a row but Jamie broke into her thoughts explaining the contents of the last phone call.

"Oh my god!" Cara said, switching off the coffee machine and turning to Ashling. "Of course you must go, please let me know what happens, I am sure it will turn out to be nothing, but if there is anything and I mean anything I can do please call me" and with that she gave them both a hug and kiss in turn.

Once in the car they were both fastening their seatbelts and thinking what the hell had happened to cause this behaviour. Ashling was racking her brains trying to remember anything she might have said to upset Helen and Jamie was thinking he always thought Helen was a bit of a nut case but not this bad. After a moment or two Jamie started the car, tuned into the local radio station and they travelled in silence.

After what seemed like an eternity, although was only just over an hour, they pulled up and parked outside Ashling and Helen's flat but before he had time to even turn off the engine Ashling had unbuckled her seatbelt, opened the door and was racing up the pathway.

"Hang on a minute" Jamie yelled and he followed as soon as he could get the hand brake on but Ashling was gone, into the front of the house and up the flight of stairs to their flat. There, piled up on the landing outside the front door were all of Ashling's possessions squashed untidily into a few cardboard boxes and some black bin liners. Her laptop was plonked on the top. She stood for a couple of seconds in total shock. She had secretly hoped that Jamie had been right and it would all have been a stupid joke but as he rushed up behind her he realised too that he was wrong. Ashling banged on the door.

"Helen, Helen!" she called but there was no reply, she tried her key but true to his word the horrible voice on Helen's phone had been right and her key no longer worked. "Helen!" Ashling tried again "Whatever is wrong, have I done anything to upset you, please talk to me" still no response. Ashling turned to Jamie in desperation, "what do I do"? Jamie rapped on the door,

"Come on Helen, this is stupid, if you have a problem with Ash or whatever I am sure we can all have a talk and sort this out" Ashling had her ear to the door and she was sure she heard a quiet sob coming from the inside.

"Listen Helen, I know you are in there, I can hear you, come on talk to me, I thought we were besties, if I have done something you must let me know so I can put it right!"

All of a sudden a voice came from behind the door, a horrible voice, the one Ashling had heard on Helen's phone.

"Just fuck the hell off you two, Helen and I are an item now and we don't need or want you around. You have your stuff now fuck off!"

Ashling and Jamie looked at each other in shock, then finding her voice Ash shouted

"Helen, I want to hear it from you not that moron, I'll go if YOU tell me you don't want me around not some prat whom you haven't even known five minutes."

Silence and then ever so quietly a tiny voice said

"Sorry Ashling, I think you should go, Tyler and I are living here now and we want to be alone."

With that Ashling started to pick up her stuff and pointed to Jamie to help. Once they were downstairs they both loaded her stuff into the back of the car and just stood looking at each other.

"What was that all about" Jamie spoke first, "who the hell is this Tyler?"

Ashling explained about how Helen had a date with him the previous week and how she had paid for everything etc. "But she said she wasn't going to see him after Saturday night , she said he was a real chump, I certainly do not believe that she has decided to move in with him. I'm frightened Jamie, I'm sure I could hear her sobbing, I'm sure he was making her say that stuff, what are we going to do?".

Jamie thought for a moment and then suggested they give it a couple of days

"We'll give her time to re think, then we'll come back and have another go at talking, then if you are still concerned we'll go to the police and see what they have to say about it, is that OK?" Jamie put a comforting arm around Ash's shoulders. Ashling wasn't totally convinced but agreed, although she was thinking to herself she might just sneak back and wait outside the flat that night just to see if they come out or maybe Tyler would, hopefully alone so she could get in to talk to Helen.

Jamie drove Ashling to her mum's house where she explained everything to her mum while Jamie unloaded her stuff.

"Of course you must stay here" Laura her mum said "Stay as long as you like, but I do find it really strange that Helen has turned like this, she always seemed a really lovely girl and you were such good friends, let's hope you can work it out although as I say you can stay here just as long as you like"

After Jamie had left Ashling told her mum of her plan to wait outside the flat and see if she could get to Helen without Tyler being around. He mother agreed that it did seem very strange but pleaded with her daughter to be careful, suggesting she should take Jamie with her. Ashling thought about it but decided he would probably think it a stupid idea and try and talk her out of it.

She had a nice day with her mum catching up on all the family gossip and when her dad got in from his work as a solicitor they had a nice family meal together. After dinner her dad went off to his study to do some work while her mum, after they had loaded the dishwasher, got herself comfy on the sofa and put one of her favourite soaps on the TV. Ashling gave her mum a quick peck on the cheek and said she would see her later. The soap had started so her mum was engrossed and just nodded.

It was only a short bus ride to the flat so Ashling was there within 25 minutes. She pulled her coat tightly around her as it was beginning to rain. She had purposely worn a dark coat with the hope that she could blend into the darkness. As she approached the flat she could see from the front window that there was a lamp on, not the big light that would normally be blazing in the early evening, well when it was her and Helen's flat anyway.

"Hmm lamps" she thought to herself "Maybe they are being romantic and I have got this all wrong" she even thought, for a nanosecond, that maybe she should just leave things alone, then suddenly the curtains were pulled across and the light dimmed even more.

She settled herself behind a little wall in the garden of an empty house opposite, it luckily had a couple of bricks missing and gave her a really clear view of the front of their house, the lounge window and the main front door. Then, a few minutes later the front door opened and a strange figure came out. She obviously wasn't sure if it was this Tyler or not but she didn't recognise him so assumed there was a good chance it was him. She watched as the figure pulled his hoodie up over his head, tucked his hands into his pockets, hunched up his shoulders and proceeded to walk down the road towards the pub.

Quick as a flash Ashling ran across the road and opened the main front door to the house, obviously he couldn't change the lock on that as the other tenants would have to know about it and get new keys. She crept up the stairs as quietly as she could just in case she was wrong about the figure and it was in fact just another of the residents. She stood outside the flat and listened at the door, no sound was coming. She knocked gently, still nothing, then again a little louder, still nothing. She tried the door handle but of course nothing then she thought she heard a slight muffled sound, a bit like a grunt, no, more like the sound you hear on a TV show or movie when somebody is gagged or has gaffer tape around their mouth. She knocked the door again; this time she was sure she heard a grunt. As she put her head nearer the door to try and listen, Nigel, the guy who lived in the flat next door, came out of his front door.

"Is there a problem?" he said making Ashling jump. "Have you forgotten you key or something?" He sounded concerned. Ashling turned and smiled ready to say no nothing like that but then she thought why not tell him, he was a nice guy, maybe her could help her get into the flat. She explained that she had been away and that Helen wasn't answering, that she had left her keys at home (she thought that was easier and quicker than explaining the truth) she kept one eye on the stairs just in case Tyler returned, although she still wasn't sure it was actually Tyler who she had seen going out of the front door.

"Well if you are worried I can probably get in for you but it will mean calling out somebody after to fix the door as I will have to break the lock to get in, is that what you want me to do?"

Ashling nodded, all the time thinking to herself please hurry up. Nigel went back inside his flat and returned, not as quickly as Ashling wanted him too but she said nothing "I expect she's fast asleep in there" he said as he was prising the door locks with a claw hammer "Heh you're not going to do me for breaking and entering are you" he quipped. Still not understanding any urgency, after all why should he, he just thought Helen was fast asleep, sleeping off a few drinks or something.

The front door opened downstairs and Ashling froze for a second before with great relief she heard the voices of two of her other neighbours chatting away as they opened the front door of their flat on the ground floor. Creak, crunch and the door flew open "Not a very strong lock Ash" Nigel was saying but Ashling heard little as she rushed into the flat. Nigel followed because it seemed like the right thing to do. They both stopped as soon as they entered the lounge and stared at the vision in front of them.

Quick as a flash Ashling had her phone in her hand and was calling 999. Nigel had rushed over to the chair that was directly in front of them, where Helen sat, tied up to it, gagged and obviously beaten severely. One of her eyes was completely closed, her nose had been bleeding and the dried blood was all over the gag and down her front. She was just about conscious. Ashling and Nigel wasted no time in untying her and very gently they lifted her onto the sofa, she was trying to speak be it was just a hoarse whisper.

"Shhhh" Ashling was saying to her and trying to remove the duck tape that was stuck to her hair and her head. "The police and ambulance will be here very soon"

Helen lifted her hand and pointed to the door and began to cry and wriggle.

"She is trying to tell us something" Nigel said.

"I can see that!" Ashling snapped and instantly regretted being so sharp, after all Nigel had been wonderful so far. "Oh I am sorry" she said, Nigel nodded he didn't seem too bothered by her remark. "I think she is trying to tell us he will be back" he said. "I will go and wait by the front door" and picking up his hammer he headed for the door of the flat .

"Oh please be careful!" Ashling shouted after him and then turning to Helen carried on stroking her hand and telling her everything was going to be fine, even though she wasn't at all sure it would be.

Nigel opened the main front door of the Victorian house where the flats were and positioned himself on the top step. From here he could see anybody coming down the street. It was a bright moon and all the street lights were working so he had a good view. Ashling had told him everything while they were releasing Helen which included the direction the person she thought was Tyler had headed off in. Concentrating on that direction Nigel spotted a figure dressed in a dark hoody and dark jeans with his hands deep into his pockets and his shoulders hunched against the wind, heading towards the house. He gripped the handle of the hammer tightly. His heart was racing. Nigel wasn't a huge man but he did play rugby, albeit not very well, he was quite robust and certainly not frightened of standing up for himself, or Helen for that matter, assuming of course it was Tyler who had done this to Helen. It had dawned on him while he was on the step there that maybe somebody else had broken in but of course that was stupid, the wounds on Helen had not been inflicted only minutes ago. The figure was approaching at quite a pace now, it was probably only about 100 metres away when a police siren broke into the silence and within seconds rounded the end of the street and headed towards the house. At this moment the figure turned away and started to walk, not run back in the opposite direction. Nigel jumped up and started after the figure just as the police car pulled up and two officers jumped out and grabbed him. Then ten seconds later the ambulance arrived.

Nigel struggled to get away from the officers who had grabbed him, shouting "He's getting away, let me go you idiots! It's him you're after and he's getting away!" he tried to free one of his hands so he could point in the direction Tyler had taken but there was no sign of him now anyway.

"Come on sir" one of the policemen holding him said "we don't want any trouble" Nigel was still struggling when one of the policeman felt the hammer Nigel had pushed into his pocket when he was going to run after Tyler. "Now what exactly were you going to do with this sir, or rather just what have you done with it?" he spoke as the paramedics had exited the ambulance and were heading up the pathway to the front door to where an ashen faced Ashling was standing.

"This way quickly" she said and pointed up the stairs to the front door of the flat, "Number 2, please hurry, come on Nigel!" she continued but she realised that poor Nigel was being held by two police officers. "What the hell?" she ran down the path. "Why are you holding Nigel?, Let him go for god's sake, he hasn't done anything, he was out here in case Tyler returned, he was waiting for you guys, now please let him go!"

The policemen both looked at one another deciding if it was safe to release him, after all they had no idea of what had happened yet but

Ashling was so adamant they let him go that they loosened their grip on him a little.

"Well we need to know just what has happened here and just who has been hurt" Mark Gregory the more senior officer took the lead, "now we must all go inside and let's see what has happened and hear the story alright, and you sir -" looking directly at Nigel "- can explain why you have..." he pointed to the hammer which was now in the possession of the other policeman.

They all entered the flat where the paramedics were examining Helen. Phil, one of the men, turned when they entered and smiled gently as Ashling went rushing over to her friend.

"I think she will be fine" he said. "She is shocked, bruised and has a big bump on the back of her head, we are going to take her with us to St Peters just so they can give her a good night's sleep and check she hasn't got concussion but I am sure she will be home tomorrow" With that he popped a blanket around her shoulders saying "Are you able to walk to the ambulance with us or would you like me to bring a wheelchair?" Helen looked towards Ashling petrified but Ashling just smiled and said she would go with her and yes they would walk. The police said they would need a statement from at least "somebody" as the poor officers still had no idea at this stage what an earth had happened or was going on. Nigel said he would go with the police and give the statement while Ashling went to the hospital.

Tyler watched from the end of the street as the police car and ambulance drove away.

"Fucking idiots", he said to himself, "haven't got a bloody clue what's going on" and then with a smile on his face he headed towards his next port of call.

CHAPTER 4

The baby was screaming for his milk when Tyler arrived at the flat where he lived with his wife in Guildford, this made him a little annoyed. Why doesn't Samantha have her boob out ready for the poor little chap, she knows how hungry he gets. Slamming the front door behind him he entered the little lounge. The baby had gone quiet and his temper suddenly disintegrated at the sight of his lovely Sam with Dylan hanging onto her left breast. Sam looked up and smiled at Tyler, she knew better than to ask him where he had been for the past couple of days, she had done so once when they were first together but after the terrible fight it had caused she had kept her thoughts and questions locked deep inside her head. She was so frightened she would lose him that she thought she would rather not know than run the risk of him leaving her for good. Tyler reached into the carrier bag he had been carrying under his jacket and removed a huge bar of Cadbury's chocolate and a bottle of red wine. It was in fact what he was taking back to Helen's but his plans had obviously changed, so he put them on the small coffee table in front of Sam and with a cheeky grin told her they were for her. Oh he knew she would never drink the wine all the while she was breast feeding but he also knew she would be grateful that he had thought of her. Her smile grew even bigger as she saw his offerings. She was used to him disappearing for hours or days even but he quite often brought her a little something and she knew she should be glad that he did want to come back to her and that he thought enough of her to buy these small things.

"How's my boy then" Tyler leaned across Sam and very gently kissed the top of the feeding baby's head, then kissed Sam's forehead. "Has he been good then sweetheart, not too much screaming then?"

"No he has been a star" Sam cooed cuddling Dylan even tighter to her bosom making the baby struggle to get free. "He only woke up twice in the night which was great" she had said the words before she had even thought and for a split second panicked just in case Tyler was going to go off on one saying that she was getting at him for not being at home but he seemed not to notice and relief washed over her like a tidal wave.

As soon as Dylan was settled and in his crib Sam went into the kitchen to prepare some dinner for them. Tyler followed her in and grabbing her from behind squeezed her breasts so hard she squealed in pain. Pushing her away his face began to change "What the fuck is wrong with you" he said "can't I play with my own wife's tits without her screaming?" he pushed her to one side and opened the cutlery draw in search of a corkscrew.

"I'm sorry" Sam began" It's just that I'm a little sore that's all, I love you touching me you know that" and with that she tried to put her arms around his waist, for a moment his face stayed angry then all of a sudden he softened and gently cupping her face in his hands kissed her firmly on the lips.

"I'm sorry darling" he said "It's just work has been so hectic lately and what with Dylan screaming a lot it gets my nerves on edge. I will try not to take it out on you. That is why I go off sometimes you know, I just need to get some peace away from screaming babies, I do love you though, both of you" Sam felt good, her man was back, he was sorry for hurting her and he had even given her a reason as to why he was away, although she did think that Dylan was only three months old and he had been doing his disappearing act for a long long time before Dylan had been born.

Sam first met Tyler about 18 months previously in a pub in Guildford. She was waiting for her friends to show up for a hen night as Coleen was getting married two weeks later but didn't want a "fun" do, just a few drinks with her close friends in The Nightingale Arms, a riverside pub frequented by all the students from the university. Sam had got there early as she wanted to get a good table and arrange with the bar staff to bring Prosecco over as soon as Coleen had settled into her seat. She was blowing up a couple of balloons just to add a little bit of fun when Tyler wandered over and asked if she needed some more puff.

Sam warmed to his handsome face instantly and within ten minutes they had blown up ten balloons, learned each other's likes and dislikes and had new drinks in front of them. Coleen and the other four girls arrived when they were half way through their new drinks and Coleen was delighted to see the balloons and even more so when the Prosecco arrived. She looked at Tyler as Sam introduced him but the look said "thank you but now piss off as this is my hen night, OK?" Tyler took the hint but wasn't too happy about leaving Sam, and the look he gave Coleen said it all.

"So who is he? " Coleen asked Sam as soon as Tyler was out of earshot "He is lovely looking I'll grant you but there is something about him, well I don't know quite what...maybe the way he looked at me, but there was certainly something that would make me very wary of him Sam. Have you known him long?"

Sam explained about the balloons, "but we got on really well, it was like we had known each other for ages within the first couple of minutes, I thought he was rather nice actually" she replied a little miffed that her friend didn't see just how cute he was.

"Well I would take care if I were you" Coleen said "there are some strange people about and just because he is good looking doesn't mean he is harmless, now can we get on with my party" she smiled broadly and poured them all a glass of bubbly. They all had a great evening, chatting about the wedding arrangements and who was going to wear what. Sam was the only bridesmaid so didn't really have a lot to say about her dress obviously so she slunk up to the bar to order another bottle or three of Prosecco. Tyler was leaning on the bar at the other side of the pub and Sam didn't notice him until the barmaid brought a gin and tonic over and pointed at Tyler who nodded and gave her a huge grin. Sam took the Prosecco back to the girls who were all still deep in conversation, about hairdos this time, and then wandered back to where Tyler was leaning.

"Fancy carrying on our conversation with a night cap when you have finished here?" he asked "I know a club not far from here where we could go, not too noisy, maybe romantic" and with that he winked. Sam's heart missed a beat, when he did that he was drop dead gorgeous. They arranged to meet as soon as the girls had called it a day. Sam almost skipped back to the table. Wow, she thought to herself, just how lucky was she meeting him tonight.

The night was great, the club was almost empty, just a guy playing the piano in the corner of the room. Tyler was the perfect gentleman. By the time they were ready to leave Sam was a little bit tipsy and falling incredibly quickly in love.

Tyler had told her he was staying with friends at that time due to his flat being redecorated and so suggested that they carry on the rest of the evening at her place. It took Sam almost a nanosecond to agree and so they flagged down a cab and before she knew it she was being carried up the stairs to her flat, then he took the key from her, opened the door and carried her inside and found the bedroom.

It wasn't the best sex she had ever had, but it certainly wasn't the worst. She put it down to her being a bit drunk, he was quite rough which she wasn't too sure about and then when he climaxed he did nothing to ensure she did the same, just climbed off and within seconds was snoring beside her. Next time she thought it will be great next time, but he is so gorgeous do I really care how good he is in bed !!!

The next morning he woke her with a cup of tea in bed. He was wearing her dressing gown which had little kittens printed on it and lots of pink bows and they both thought it hilarious as he paraded around the bedroom pretending to be a model.

"Can I come back tonight?" he asked her. "What I mean is I would really like to come back here tonight" he winked that melting wink again and of course Sam said yes.

Well he did come back that night, and the next and the next and by the weekend he had moved in. "But what about your flat" Sam had asked him "Do you rent it or own it? I mean, suppose it doesn't work with us...it has been so fast" but Tyler just smiled and told her that "Of course it was going to work", and that "he did own his flat but he had spoken to his friend that morning and his friend had agreed to rent it from him so it wouldn't get squatters or anything" Sam was delighted, she had the man of her dreams and he had moved in!

Within five months Sam was pregnant. When she told Tyler his face was just what she hoped it would be, the smile was honest, he was really excited and she was over the moon too. The very next day Tyler came home from work with a ring for Sam saying that the next day they would be going to the register office to arrange their wedding. Sam had hoped for a proper proposal as all girls would, but she was so swept along with Tyler's enthusiasm that she just said "Great, what time?"

They were married two weeks later, just a very quiet affair. Sam only told her parents as she said she couldn't get married without them being there. At first they were really shocked but could see how happy Sam was so they attended. Tyler didn't invite anybody. Sam's parents were the witnesses and then off they went for a curry. They invited her parents but they said they had plans, this upset Sam but she was just so happy to be Mrs Sam Brooker. She just gave each of them a hug and let them go. Tyler shook hands with them both and promised to look after their daughter.

Sam and Tyler's life was good on the surface but Sam was concerned that she knew very little of Tyler's past or what he did for work, where his parents lived, if he had brothers or sisters. She broached the subject on many occasions but he always fobbed her off with different excuses. Parents are dead so didn't want to talk about them, work was really hectic and didn't want to discuss it and make them miserable, excuse after excuse so eventually Sam gave up.

It was about half way through her pregnancy that Tyler started to stay out overnight. It was just the odd night to begin with then started to increase to maybe two or three nights. The first few times Sam was really worried in case he had had an accident and was lying in hospital or even dead somewhere. His mobile always went to voicemail on these occasions. On the second time he was away for three nights Sam was so desperate she called the police. They sent an officer round to the flat and while he was there Tyler came home. The policeman had been friendly and understanding when Tyler explained he had had to suddenly go away for work and had no battery on his phone, although he did say he should have found a way to call his wife. Tyler started to get angry at this point saying it was none of his business, the policeman calmed him but glanced at Sam with a look that said "I don't believe it for one minute"

Once he had gone the row that ensued convinced Sam never to say anything about his disappearing acts ever again. She was so besotted with the guy and anyway she had more to worry about with a baby on the way.

The policeman went back to the station and wrote up his report, although there was nothing special to write he did mark it as a possible "problem domestic" in the future. Then it was filed.

Having a wife and a baby had changed Tyler or so he had thought. Oh he would go off on a few nights shagging with any old trollop, as he liked to think of them, who was up for some rough sex. He had stopped being as rough with Sam as she had said she didn't like it so pleasing her had become important. He was sure he loved her so bonking elsewhere became a sort of hobby, after all he was actually doing her a favour by not taking his roughness out on her wasn't he!

Things changed the night he met Helen. There was an instant attraction, also he was hungry and broke and fancied some food, sex and fun. It didn't quite work out the way he had planned. He was convinced he would be invited back to her place but she had made it clear in the Indian Restaurant that she would be in her bed alone that night so he had a quick change of plan.

Sam had been pleased to see Tyler arrive home as she was fully expecting him to be having one of his disappearing acts as the baby had been playing up quite lot that day. She went to hug him as he came in but could see instantly by the scowl on his face that he was in a foul mood and she knew better than to attempt to make any moves towards him so she just held back and asked if he would like something to eat or drink before they went to bed.

Almost instantly his face softened when he heard the cooing of Dylan in the nursery and went straight in to pick up his son. Sam watched from the door and wondered just what made her husband tick. From anger to softness in just seconds. Once he had settled Dylan he followed Sam into the kitchen where he declined food but agreed to a night cap of a small whiskey. They lay in bed, neither touching the other. Sam wanting to snuggle tight with her husband and Tyler thinking just how was he going to see Helen again after making her pay for their evening. Stop it, his brain kept telling him, you have a wife and child now, you are no longer *Simon*, but his brain had already started to take over.......Tyler he kept telling it....no you are *Simon* it kept replying !!!!!.

The day after Tyler had attacked Helen and returned to the loving arms of his totally innocent wife he decided he was going to change. He decided he was no longer going to listen to his "mad brain...*Simon*"...he had actually named his brain when it was experiencing it's madness, well he had used the name on so many occasions he had got quite used to it and it now almost felt like a friend, well an evil friend if such a friend could exist. Tyler was now his real name he had decided on it long ago but when *Simon* took over...well he had no control as *Simon* was a far stronger character than Tyler ever was. Oh yes Tyler could be cruel, moody and even dangerous at times but nowhere near as much as *Simon*. Once *Simon* took control even Tyler was frightened.

CHAPTER 5

Tyler, or *Simon*, or whoever he was actually born as, was a child born with multiple personalities. He was never diagnosed with any problems as he had learned from a very early age that he could manage his different personalities and show just what people wanted to see.

He was adopted by a nice middle aged couple called Elise and Brendan Murdoch who lived in Brighton. They had not been able to have any children of their own and were ecstatic to have the opportunity to love and protect Tyler.

Tyler's birth mother had died of a drug overdose or accidental overload as it was really, and his natural father had never been identified. He had a supposedly happy childhood with his adoptive family and nobody seemed to be aware of his problems, even Tyler himself. He knew he was different, he knew that strange ideas came into his head, he knew he could be very angry but didn't know why. He felt that there was another person in his head that made feelings just creep up on him and then his head would almost explode. He knew he would kill people one day although he had no idea when or who or why but the thought excited him and he spent many a night locked in his bedroom planning how he would kill and how he would get away with it.

It started when he was just sixteen. His was just normal Tyler then. He had been at a school disco and had asked Jenny Phillips for a dance. She was not the prettiest girl in the school and he had felt a bit sorry for her as nobody had asked her to dance and she looked a bit sad, but when he asked her she had just laughed at him and said she was fed up and not hard up! Tyler had pushed her against the wall and stormed off to the boy's toilets leaving her in tears and rubbing her shoulder where he had pushed her.

He locked himself into one of the cubicles, and sat fully clothed on the loo. No toilet seats in schools in those days and he jumped up quickly as he realised he had got something wet on his trousers, looking down he realised it was piss on the surface of the toilet, dirty gits he thought. Suddenly he started to get a strange and violent headache, a voice began to shout in his head, get them, get them all, the bastards. *Simon* had woken in his head and his anger told him somebody must be punished.

There was no stopping him once he had stirred and very soon *Simon* was in total control and Tyler's headache disappeared, he felt great. He was becoming *Simon*!

He waited outside the school gates until the disco had ended and everybody was filing out. Jenny was with another two girls but they both had boys in tow and she looked like a spare part. He walked far enough behind them so as not to be seen, hiding behind hedges if any of them turned for any reason. After about half a mile the two friends were getting far into the boys, cuddling and kissing as they walked along, eventually one of the boys said to Jenny it was about time she buggered off and went her own way. The girls protested but only half heartedly as they just wanted to be alone with the boys. Jenny took the hint and walked off in a different direction. It was a much longer way for her to walk home but she didn't care. She had had a rotten night, wished she had never bothered to go to the stupid dance anyway, it was only Ruthie and Gayle who had persuaded her and now they had dumped her for the boys. She knew it would happen but she didn't get many offers to go out so had jumped at their invitation for her to go with them to the disco. The poor girl so rarely had fun, she had even thought that maybe they were going to be friends with her. What she didn't know was that their parents had said they must offer to take her as Jenny's mum had mentioned to them that she never went out and how nice it would be if either Ruthie or Gayle suggested she went with them. Of course the girls had protested as they thought of Jenny as the class geek but had agreed eventually from parental pressure.

Tyler, or rather *Simon*, watched her as she walked away from the others and followed, still a safe distance behind. He had no idea where Jenny lived but he guessed it wasn't too far from the school so he knew he would have to be quick if he wanted to carry out his plan. As luck would have it, for *Simon* at any rate, Jenny lived the other side of a huge patch of wasteland. There were several tall trees and simply loads of bushes dotted around with a wide pathway running through the middle. He could see the lights of the houses in the distance at the end of the path so it didn't give him much time. He began to quicken his pace and didn't notice a strand of gorse, he caught his foot and went down with a bump shouting in anger as he went.

"Fuck! Fuck! Fuck" Jenny turned and realised somebody was behind her but instead of running away she went to help him up. If only she had run.

"Oh my god are you OK ?" she said, then realising it was Tyler she began to turn away but *Simon*'s plan was already in place in his head and he wasn't going to change it now.

"Wait!" he shouted "I was following you so I could apologise for pushing you earlier and I wanted to see you got home safely." He put on his "special smile"

Jenny turned back and said "I'm sorry too, I didn't mean to be mean to you I was just shocked you asked me to dance that's all, I thought you were taking the piss out of me" she smiled and Tyler almost changed his mind but *Simon* was in his head and said *go on you know what you want to do, go on you've planned this now, go on, go on, GO ON* !!!! For the next 20 minutes Tyler completely disappeared and *Simon* took over.

He got back to his house a little after midnight, his parents were well asleep by then so he had no problems with stripping off his clothes and stuffing them into a bin liner, which he then double and the treble bagged and secured with the ties provided and stashed well under his bed in an old suitcase. He went into the bathroom and showered, worrying for a few moments in case his parents woke up with the sound of the shower running but then he smiled to himself, as if they would ever wake up, world war three could break out and they would sleep through it he thought but he waited for a few seconds before getting into the shower just to check. Yes he could hear his father's snores over the sound of the running water so he got in. A few minutes later he was in his bedroom, dry, clean and so very hyper. His excitement of what he had done was coursing through his veins like a drug. But as with all drugs, the comedown is not quite so euphoric and an hour or so later he found himself crying into his pillow. He was Tyler, the good boy and not *Simon* the fiend, what had he done....this feeling lasted until his mother called up the stairs for him to hurry up and get ready or he would be late for school. *Simon* was slowly creeping back into his head.

As soon as he got to the school gates he knew Jenny had been found. He thought it might take a little longer to find her as he had covered her in all the loose leaves he could collect together in the dark and in his hurry, but her parents must have been waiting up and when she didn't come home they must have searched. The talk of the "finding" was all over the playground. Everybody wanting to be involved in what they thought had happened and who saw her last, all dying to be important by giving information to the police who had just arrived and were with the teachers ushering everyone into the school hall. Maybe, Tyler thought to himself, if anybody had cared that much about poor Jenny she wouldn't have been walking home alone anyway the stupid, uncaring idiots.

It took several weeks of police investigations for them to conclude that they had nothing concrete to go on. The postmortem had shown that Jenny had been raped but there was no DNA as the rapist must have worn gloves and used a condom, none of which was found. She was then, it was thought knocked unconscious and then suffocated, possibly by the murderer sitting on her face until she had stopped breathing.

They had interviewed each and every one of the pupils who were at the disco the night Jenny died but to no avail. They had all seen Jenny walking home but nobody had seen her since she had rounded the corner towards the wasteland. Tyler had put on a real show of sadness and pity, almost in tears as he explained how he had begged Jenny to let him walk her home but she had refused. Even to the extent of one of the police women mentioning to her colleague how sensitive the lad was and it was such a shame that she hadn't taken him up on his offer.

Tyler didn't have any more thoughts of remorse after that first night, in fact he was getting more and more excited about his next *event* as he had decided to name it. He had dispensed of his clothes in the school incinerator explaining to the caretaker that is was a bag of old gym clothes they had cleared out of the lockers in the boys changing rooms. He was very smug as it had been so very easy. He considered himself the star of the show and couldn't wait to plan the next one.

Well the planning of his next *event* didn't come that soon for Tyler as he suddenly found himself, for no apparent reason, the centre of attention in his class, even his year, maybe even his school. All the girls suddenly wanted to be his girlfriend and lots of the boys wanted to be his best pal. Tyler had never known such attention. Maybe it was that he had been so sad for poor Jenny and her demise and that he had shown so much remorse that he hadn't persuaded her to let him walk her home in safety. When he thought of that and all the respect he was getting from his peers he would secretly smile to himself and pat himself on the back to think he had fooled the suckers, but he also felt a little sad that it had taken something as bad as that to make people like him, although that last thought was only a very brief one!

Another reason everyone had suddenly taken a shine to him might have had something to with his incredible good looks that were beginning to emerge even more now that he was almost seventeen. Gone was the acne that had plagued him through his early teens, gone was the pale gaunt look he had always supported even though at one stage he had even tried to cover his face with a light dusting of his mother's face powder. There was no doubt that he was a very handsome young man and it was noticed by everyone, even the teachers.

Tyler learned this during one of his geography lessons when Miss Thomas asked him to stay after the end of the lessons to help tidy away some of the maps and globes she had been using during the class. As the other boys had filed out of the room a couple of them had turned and winked at him as if to say "Lucky bastard, get in there". Well he almost did but they were interrupted by one of the other teachers opening the door to the store cupboard. When he got home that night he went straight to his bedroom, locked the door and with his penis in his hand laid back and thought about Miss Thomas.

The rest of his seventeenth year was mostly taken up with his new found interest in geography. He always insisted in staying after school to help out, sorting out the maps and putting away anything that needed to go into the store cupboard. It all came to a crushing end though when at the end of term Miss Thomas announced she was going to be Mrs Cramer and was moving away to Scotland with her new husband.

Tyler was sad but not for too long because a girl called Cindy had started to become a little bit closer than just one of the gang he went around with. He had been on dates with several of the girls but nobody had actually made any real impact on him. On his eighteenth birthday Cindy had made a play for him and wow was she hot!. He had been told to meet the gang in the local pub at 7.30pm for his birthday bash, he had been on his way when Cindy had ambushed him, strangely enough it was very close to where he had murdered Jenny. Of course Cindy didn't know this as she had only been at the school for the past six months. They lay on the grass under the tree where poor Jenny had taken her last breath. Tyler was so excited by the thought of this and of course the hot Cindy laying with him that he hardly had time to get her knickers down before he had climaxed. She thought it was all due to her being so sexy and was delighted that she could turn the wonderful Tyler on so fast, if only she had known.

CHAPTER 6

Tyler quite enjoyed hanging around with Cindy. He also enjoyed all the looks he got from the other girls as they were all vying for his attention. He was clearly the best looking boy in the school so when it came to prom day he had his pick. He was going to take Cindy of course, or so she thought but a couple of weeks before the big night they had a row about just what mode of transport they would use to get to the prom. Cindy wanted a horse drawn carriage to Tyler's disgust, he said it would be a hired Limo or nothing. Cindy had sulked for a day or so and then relented, but it was too late as Tyler had already asked Janie Beacons. She was not in the same league as Cindy in the looks or boobs department but seemed like she was quite happy to have sex with Tyler as she had already dropped several hints. He thought that would teach Cindy a lesson. Truth be told he was getting a bit too fond of the girl and his original plan to allow *Simon* a free rein on her had started to lessen.

Prom day arrived. Tyler and Cindy hadn't been out or even spoken since he told her he was taking Janie to the prom. He was a little sad and missed her and the feel of her great boobs pushing up against him when they made love but he knew he was in for a good night with Janie as she had given out so many hints. Cindy had decided not to go to the prom which made Tyler feel a bit guilty, a feeling he didn't much like, he certainly wasn't used to having any types of real feelings and it disturbed him a bit. Slowly he allowed *Simon* to emerge and once he was out any feelings of remorse disappeared.

The prom was as expected, all glam, giggles, and posh cars. It was nothing special, just a big build up and a damp squib as far as Tyler was concerned but he was looking forward to the after prom time, when he would eventually get a chance to fuck the daylights out of Janie.

The dance finished and everyone started to go their separate ways, either home or to after parties. Janie grabbed Tyler's hand and pulled him to one side of the entrance hall as people filed past. She started to kiss him but just as he felt his prick moving in his trousers Tim Proctor butted his head around the corner and shouted, "Come on you two, we are all off to Pete's house, he is holding an after party in one of his dads old barns, the whole gang are coming".

Tyler was just about to tell Tim to piss off when Janie spun round and shouted "Brilliant, we're on our way" and with that she pulled away from Tyler, grabbed his hand again and led the way to where Tim was waiting. Tyler was not impressed but thought he would go along anyway, maybe they could find somewhere at Pete's farm, away from the others for their shag. Everyone piled into an old van one of the boys had borrowed. The farm was only about ten minutes drive away but all Tyler could think about was the stirring in his pants and just what he was going to do to Janie once they arrived and found a secluded spot. Those ten minutes seemed like an eternity. Eventually they arrived and all climbed out. During the journey Janie had been touching Tyler's crotch and he was so ready for some fun that he was out of the van in a second and with Janie in tow, and started to head for the wooded side of the barn, but just as they had taken their second step Tim appeared, "Come on guys, it's this way" he said rather too sharply. He knew exactly what was happening but was doing his utmost to stop it as he was really keen on Janie. They had been an item for a short time a few months before but once Tyler had become the boy of the moment with the girls Janie had dropped him and given Tyler the eye instead. Although he was with Cindy she had hung around until he noticed her and her obvious intentions. Tim was still hoping he could win her back if he kept her away from Tyler.

Janie looked a bit embarrassed as she knew exactly what Tim had thought they were up to so she attempted to drop Tyler's hand and turned to go back towards the others but Tyler kept a tight grip on her. He turned to Tim and with a snarl in his voice told him to fuck the hell off and leave them alone. Tim looked a bit taken aback but turned and headed back towards the others. "Aw come on Tyler" Janie said "he didn't mean anything by it, he just wanted us to join the gang" she was a bit frightened by the tone in Tyler's voice.

Tyler stared at the girl standing before him. All of a sudden he wanted to kill her. All of a sudden his desire to see her die was so strong. *Simon* had completely taken over. He tightened his grip on her hand and started pulling her towards a clump of bushes behind the barn, Janie pulled against him and in a timid voice suggested they go back with the others as they might be missing a lot of fun. All of a sudden all her bravado ebbed away and fear started to take over but Tyler was having none of it. He pulled hard at her, almost dragging her towards the bushes. *Simon* was well and truly active now and nothing was going to stop him.

Suddenly out of nowhere came a horrendous scream. Even Tyler stopped dead in his tracks. All of a sudden everyone was moving around looking for the source of the scream. Tyler had let go of Janie for an instant and she was now rushing to join the others. She was lost amongst them instantly and *Simon* resigned himself to the fact that nothing was going to happen with her tonight now.

The blood curdling scream had happened just at the right time for Janie, little did she know that this was her lucky night.

As it turned out the scream had been one of the girls coming face to face with a dead badger. It might have been lucky for Janie but when Tyler saw her later cuddled up next to Tim sitting around the bonfire with the others he had a change of plan. *Simon* had decided that somebody was still going to die tonight.

He walked away from the party, to the disappointment of some of the girls who had thought they might be in with a chance once Janie had obviously decided to be with Tim. They watched him leave but said nothing when they heard Tim say good riddance.

Tyler was really annoyed as he climbed through the fence at the end of the field, he was heading for the lane that led back to the town and home when again *Simon* pushed his way back into place and asked Tyler what the bloody hell he was doing. He had plans for tonight so why was he going home without finishing what he had set out to do. OK so Janie was out of the picture for tonight but that didn't mean his plan to kill had to change. There were plenty more fish in the sea or rather in the centre of town where he found himself now headed.

He got to Mario's, the local Pizzeria about midnight. It was still quite full as due to the relaxed licensing laws it could serve alcohol until whatever time, so the local students and teenagers would pile in and share some dough sticks so they could drink beer for as long as possible.

Tyler stood in the car park, which was almost empty due to the customers all being far too young to own cars and far too young to drink beer, but Mario turned a blind eye to their ages as he was making a nice little earner charging twice what he should for a bottle of Pils or Budweiser. He often wondered where these youngsters got their money but heh what the hell did he care as long as they paid his prices.

At the far end of the car park was an old half brick half tin building that had once been the store room for the previous owners business of a small hardware shop but the shed was now almost derelict. The door to the front was hanging off its hinges but the roof was still intact and it was dry inside. Tyler walked inside and *Simon* told him , yes this is just perfect.

At around a quarter to one the bar started to empty out, several of the girls were attached to their boyfriends arms but one or two of them came out alone. Tyler's eyes were immediately drawn to a dark haired girl who stood alone. Small and slim, wearing a really short denim skirt and a tee shirt with some writing on the front but Tyler was too far away to see exactly what the words said. She had a cardigan loosely drooping, the look that a lot of young girls went for, where the sleeves almost cover the hands and the neck sort of falls from the shoulders. She looked about sixteen or seventeen but she could easily have been a lot younger as she had so much makeup on he could see it from where he watched. Tonight's target *Simon* whispered in Tyler's head and a smile began to reach his lips. Be patient he thought, just in case she is waiting for a boyfriend or another girl, but tonight was a lucky night for Tyler, not so lucky for Ami though!!!!!

The crowd soon dispersed leaving the girl standing alone, she was a little drunk Tyler thought as he noticed her stagger when she tried to get her bearings. She looked both left and right then amazingly started to walk towards the shed and Tyler. This is far too easy, Tyler thought, she is walking straight into me, but just before she got to the door a voice called out across the car park. It was another girl calling "Ami where are you, are you out here, come on it's time to go home". Ami was just close enough for Tyler to reach out and grab her, which he did in a flash, forcing his hand over her mouth as he pulled her into the building. She didn't put up too much of a struggle as she had obviously had a lot more to drink that Tyler had at first thought. Another voice called out into the darkness, "Come on Ami where the hell are you" then a second voice, a boy this time shouting "Come on you stupid bitch, I didn't mean to say those things, we have to get home or mum will be going frantic", then another voice, "Aw come on she's probably on her way home now anyway, she's not out here" and with that all went quiet, well with the exception of a now panicking breathing noise coming from under Tyler's hand.

He only had to punch her once to quieten her. Her nose was broken instantly and her breathing became desperate as she tried to swallow the blood that was hitting the back of her throat. She struggled against his arm but to no avail. Suddenly her fight for survival took over and she started calm down and reason with whoever it was that was holding her. She had sobered up as soon as the blood and pain of her broken nose hit her senses. "If you want sex it's OK" she started to say, "I won't tell anybody I promise, I don't know who you are so I can't recognise you, please just do it and let me go"

"Fucking slut!" was all she got in reply and another punch which this time knocked several of her teeth to the back of her throat and she started to choke. Very calmly Tyler put his hand tightly over her mouth and within a couple of minutes she had stopped struggling and lay limp in his arms.

He lay her on the floor and looked down on her still body. It wasn't too bad a body, skirt much too short, just the sort a tart would wear when she was asking for sex but she had nice pert boobs which he loved the feel of. He guessed it had been a while since she had been a virgin and quickly decided to arm himself with a condom before removing all her clothes and having sex with her while her body was still warm.

He left her body in the shed knowing that it wouldn't be found for a few hours at least which gave him plenty of time to check he had left no evidence of ever being there.

The adrenalin coursing through his body as he walked home was amazing. It was like he had taken some incredible drug and was as high as possible. He wasn't that high though that he didn't take a lot of care not to be seen on his way, if he spotted anybody in the distance he hid in the shadows. By the time he was home his elation had turned into smug conceit. Inside his head *Simon* was laughing at the stupid bitch who had got herself drunk and killed totally by her own stupidity.

Tyler slept like a log, no remorse feelings, *Simon* had squashed any that might have been bubbling on the surface of his thoughts. *Simon* was getting stronger and stronger and Tyler loved it.

The following morning there was no school as the prom was the end of the term so Tyler didn't bother to get up until his mother called him to tell him lunch was ready. He wandered downstairs looking exactly as he felt, smug. His mother noticed his face was not so angry or down for once and mentioned that he must have had a great night as he looked so happy. He walked over to her and gave her a hug which was totally out of character but she warmed to it immediately and hugged him back until *Simon* nudged Tyler in the back of his brain and made him pull away saying "OK that's enough, where's this lunch then?"

Simon did not like Tyler to be "normal" he was fixing him exactly where he wanted him and wasn't going to let any mushy stuff creep back into him. Sadly his mother let him go and turned to put his lunch on the table.

In the kitchen there was a little TV which, although was turned on, the sound had been turned down. As Tyler began to eat he noticed the local news had just come on. "Turn the TV up mum" he said, his mother gave him a look that said how about a please but he ignored it, just stared at her until she turned it up. There was nothing about a body being found, nothing about anybody missing, he was not too surprised as she was in that shed which was probably only looked in once in a blue moon and as she was just a tart her parents probably won't worry about her not coming home for a while.

Just as the news was finishing the newsreader was handed a sheet of paper which she read out. "The police are anxious to know the whereabouts of Ami Saddler. She was last seen at the Mario's pizzeria last evening but has not been seen since. He brother said he saw her walk out of the restaurant but didn't see her again. Thinking she had walked home he didn't worry until this morning when he realised she hadn't come home. Her parents Molly and Sean Saddler are appealing for any information. They said she wasn't the type of girl that would just go off without telling anybody"

Yeah right, thought Tyler, she was just an old slag but as he listened to the newsreader she was saying just how bright and clever Ami was, she had apparently been accepted by three different universities as her exam results had been so good. She wanted to train as a doctor, they said. She was not the kind of girl to just disappear. For a nanosecond Tyler felt a tiny bit of remorse but *Simon* soon squashed that feeling. She was drunk and staggering after all and she had offered him sex, so just how angelic was she eh!!!!

The news ended with a plea for anybody with information to come forward.

“Oh I hope she gets home safely, her parents must be frantic” his mother was saying but Tyler just grunted and left the kitchen.

He got his coat and headed off to the shopping centre expecting to find Cindy working in the Costa Coffee bar on the first floor, he thought he might apologise for being a git and taking Janie to the prom, thought maybe she might give him some sex if he was nice to her again but she wasn’t there. He got a coffee anyway and sat in one of the booths. After five minutes or so a few of his friends from school came in and joined him. “How did you make out with Janie last night then” they asked him. None of them had gone on the after party so wouldn’t have known what happened with Janie and Tim.

“Didn’t bother in the end” Tyler told them.

“We bet, did she blow you out then?” one of the boys asked and they all started to laugh. Normally Tyler would have let it go but today he decided he didn’t want the banter so he made his excuses about having to meet his father to look at a car for him. This impressed them all, fancy his dad buying him a car, so with envy in their eyes he left them to it.

He strolled around the shopping centre for a few minutes longer than decided to head for home. As he walked outside he spotted Cindy just heading in for her shift at the coffee bar.

She hadn’t seen him so he stayed behind some shoppers who were looking longingly and discussing a really nice sofa in the window of John Lewis. He waited until she was almost at the coffee bar when he headed off in pursuit. He stood at the counter and waited until she came out from the back tying her uniform apron as she walked. She spotted Tyler immediately and her face lit up. Then just as quickly it turned into a scowl, as if she had just remembered that they weren't an item any more. Tyler wasn't going to let this put him off so he just stood there until she had to come over to serve him.

"Yes" she said very abruptly. She didn't follow with "and what can I get you today sir" as she would have done to any other customer. Tyler was a little put out, he thought that once she saw him that she would soften and want to be with him as before, but she was obviously having none of it. "Regular flat white please" he said. She just looked straight at him at which point Tyler did what he would always do when in a corner and in trouble with a woman, he turned on the smile, the special Tyler smile. It took all of five seconds for Cindy to continue her scowl but then looking at his smile her heart melted and she smiled back. As she turned to get his coffee he pulled out a sign from his pocket that he had made earlier, unfolded it and held it up like somebody would do at an airport when they are picking up a stranger, it said "SORRY CINDY" in big bold letters, her face said it all when she saw it, she had her man back and he was sorry.

They arranged to meet at Cindy's house after her shift had finished so Tyler left giving her one of his special winks as he left. Once outside he didn't know quite what to do with the day as Cindy wouldn't be finished for hours yet. He strolled around the shopping mall thinking to himself that maybe, just maybe, Cindy was the girl for him. After all she did look quite sexy in her apron and was obviously so happy to be back with him. He smiled to himself as he pictured taking her down to the river bank where there was a nice secluded glade and he could have the much awaited sex with her. Still with this thought in his head *Simon* started to stir.

What the fuck are you thinking, he said she's just another whore, you are surely not going to waste your time on a whore are you?

Tyler walked to Mario's, the pizzeria where he had seen to the decline of poor Ami. He didn't obviously go near the shed at the back of course.

Once inside he took a seat near the window and watched as customers came and went, totally unaware that Ami Saddler was in the shed behind them and decomposing as they drank their beers and ate their pizzas. He felt smug, almost cocky. He wanted to tell somebody, he wanted to brag about just how clever he was. How he could commit murder and get away with it. How nobody had ever suspected him. But of course he must never do such a thing. *Simon* was getting stronger all the time now and Tyler could feel his power overtaking his good side, his once sensible side. The urge to kill again was getting stronger almost by the hour.

He ordered a medium pizza and a beer and ate hungrily once it arrived. He was beginning to feel excited which had made him hungry. He wasn't yet sure if the excitement was because he was going to meet Cindy later and get a shag or whether it was *Simon's* influence telling him another death was imminent. He ordered a second beer and started to feel more relaxed. *Simon* had gone quiet so Tyler could concentrate on just how he was going to get Cindy to cooperate in the glade tonight. He guessed she would be fine but as he had discovered in the past you can never take a woman for granted. He decided he did like Cindy and he was going to ask her to go steady regardless of what *Simon* was going to tell him; maybe they would end up getting married someday. He could do a lot worse he thought. Then *Simon* woke up.

Tyler arrived at Cindy's house just after she got home from the cafe.

"Wow you're keen" she said as she opened the door to him, "I haven't had my dinner yet" Tyler just smiled and leaned forward to plant a kiss on her lips when her mother came into the hall.

"Oh it's you" she said scornfully "I thought you two had parted company" and at that she turned and went back into the kitchen.

"Your mum has never liked me" Tyler complained

"Arr it's just that she doesn't know you and she saw how upset I was about the prom. She'll come around once we're married" For a split second Tyler thought she was serious but then realised, as she burst out laughing, that it was a joke. "You should have seen your face" she laughed, but Tyler didn't think it was so funny, he didn't like being laughed at. He didn't like that at all!

Cindy wolfed her dinner down while Tyler sat at the kitchen table watching her. Her mum had, grudgingly, Tyler supposed, offered him something to eat too but he declined saying he had just eaten. Although he had eaten nothing since his pizza at lunch time and could easily have murdered (strange choice of words he thought) a piece of quiche and some chips like he was watching Cindy gobble down as if she hadn't eaten for days. He wasn't going to give her mum the satisfaction of having to feed her daughter's so called boyfriend. The feeling of dislike was as strong with Tyler as it was with Cindy's mum so no love lost there.

"Come on hurry up" Tyler said after twenty minutes. Seeing how she gobbled up her dinner had given him ideas and his trousers were becoming tighter as his penis was starting to swell. Get your jaws around this he was thinking as he gently touched himself under the table. But Cindy was having none of it, her mother had taken away her dinner plate and presented her with a huge bowl of apple crumble and custard. This was all too much for Tyler and he stood and started to pace, "Aw come on now Cindy" he said again "You've eaten enough, you'll get fat". At this comment her mother turned on him.

"Now just you shut up" she almost shouted the words "You should have come at a later time, my Cindy has been working which is more than I can say for you, and she needs her dinner. She will not get fat, now just go and wait for her somewhere else you little shit"

"Mum" Cindy squealed "please don't be so awful, he was only joking weren't you Tyler, he's just keen to go out"

"Don't bother" Tyler said and with that he walked from the house as fast as he could, hands tucked into his jeans pockets where he could feel his penis was now flaccid.

"Bloody bitch" *Simon* said as Tyler stomped down the road. Cindy was shouting after him but he didn't turn around. I told you she wasn't for you, you idiot, he continued but for once Tyler replied. I'm not mad at Cindy, it's that mother of hers that has wound me up. In that second he suddenly realised that on occasions he could actually answer *Simon* and even quieten him. Maybe he wasn't completely out of control after all, well in this instance anyway.

Once he was at the end of the road he waited for Cindy. He knew she would follow him as soon as she had run back into her house and pulled on a coat and shoes. He felt a bit sorry as she probably won't have finished her apple crumble after all and this made him smile. Five minutes later she arrived.

"Oh I'm so glad you waited" she said "I was worried you had gone home and wouldn't want to see me, I am sorry about my mum, she is just very protective of me you know. I'm sure your mum would be the same if you were a girl"

This thought made Tyler smile, "I wonder what I would have been like as a girl" he said.

Cindy just touched his crotch and said "I'm glad you're not" and winked. His "friend" was in motion again and his jeans started to tighten. He took her hand and led her at a fast walk towards the river and a clearing where Tyler had played as a child.

The glade was just as Tyler remembered, well apart from a few more nettles, but this was not a problem, he took off his jacket and laid it down for Cindy to lie on. She was kissing him as he laid her down and the promise of what was in store was almost prodigious. She was pulling at the belt of his jeans just as a voice came floating through the glade.

"Cindy, Cindy!" it was calling "Cindy please where are you"? There was such panic in the voice it made Cindy immediately stop pulling at his belt and pushing him off as she sat up.

"That's my mum!" she squealed "Something must be wrong for her to come looking for me"

"How the bloody hell did she know you would be here?" Tyler was not amused, this bloody woman was ruining his intentions and she was beginning to get on his nerves. It didn't occur to his over sexed self that there might actually be something wrong, all he could think of was that his evening was being fucked with.

Cindy was up now and straightening her clothes. "I had better go" she said "My mum wouldn't come looking for me if it wasn't important. She must have guessed we'd probably going for a walk down here." Yes, thought Tyler, I bet she guessed why as well and has come to spoil my fun.

Cindy turned, and giving him an apologetic shrug, headed off, not even looking back at Tyler who was getting angrier by the second. *Simon* was awake and in a very bad mood. *Let the bitch go he said she's not worth the bother, what do you care about her or her mother.*

Tyler stood for a few minutes trying to decide whether to follow Cindy or not when suddenly from behind a bush her mother appeared.

"Where is Cindy?" she screamed at him, she looked terrified as if she was going to self combust Tyler thought to himself and as he did so *Simon* started to smile from within.

"What the bloody hell is wrong with you" Tyler said sneering "Cindy isn't here, she's gone looking for you!" But before she had a chance to explain *Simon* urged Tyler to grab the hysterical woman and push her violently towards the river, then as she stumbled back she fell and went crashing down onto a tree stump hitting her head hard. Tyler just looked on while *Simon* took over again and using Tyler's left foot kicked the unconscious woman into the water. Well done *Simon* told him as Tyler walked away feeling really rather satisfied.

Talk of the terrible accident of Cindy's mother drowning after slipping whilst searching for her daughter filled all the local papers the following day. Apparently some dog walkers saw a body floating a mile or so further down the river. Making it even more tragic was the fact that her reason for searching for her daughter was to tell her that her father had been rushed into hospital with a suspected heart attack. All this news was followed the next day with news of the discovery of a partly decomposed corpse, suspected to be that of Ami Saddler, in a shed behind a local pizzeria.

All of this was of no interest to Tyler as the day after the incident with Cindy he left the area.

He left a note for his parents saying he was going travelling. He packed a backpack, stole his mother's savings that she kept hidden, or she supposed she had kept hidden, from an old shoe box at the back of her wardrobe. Stupid bitch, Tyler had thought when he rummaged in the most obvious place anybody would hide anything of value. He also found a diamond ring in the box. He knew it was valuable as his mother had inherited it from her grandmother but never wore it as it was a little large and she was frightened she would lose it. Well she has lost it now he chuckled to himself.

Slamming the front door behind him he almost skipped down the road, he was free.

CHAPTER 7

Tyler's new life was about to begin.

He got on a number 24 bus at the local bus station in Brighton, he purposefully didn't even look at its final destination. He thought it would be a good omen if it terminated somewhere that he might like to be. It didn't. He ended up at a terminus just outside Dorking. Now Dorking in itself is a rather nice moderate town in Surrey, that part was fine, but, after looking around for somewhere to stay at a reasonable cost, he soon realised it was far too expensive. He headed for the train station and settled himself on platform 1. He decided if it went in a westerly direction or at least away from the London outskirts, he was sure he would be able to find somewhere cheaper. Once on the train he heard the announcer say to change for Aldershot at the next station. Well at least he had heard of Aldershot although not why he had but thought that might be a good bet anyway.

He arrived at three in the afternoon, it was pouring with rain and so miserable that he thought he might just get on the next train home but dismissed this thought immediately, knowing that if he went back there could be questions asked, if not by the police, then certainly by Cindy, and he wasn't going to get drawn into anything that might link him to the deaths.

He wandered around the town for a while until he was soaked through and getting really cold. He had looked in a few shop windows where they advertised items for sale and hopefully lodgings etc. but he only found a piano that was out of tune and for sale for 20 pounds, buyer to collect, and a Delia, who offered massages at rates depending on what type of massage required plus a discount for anyone in the armed forces. This had made Tyler smile. He knew it was a military town once but didn't think it was now, so he wondered just how long the advert had been in the window.

He was getting fed up so headed for a greasy spoon cafe he had noticed near the station. He ordered a cup of coffee and a bacon sandwich and took a seat in the corner behind the door so he didn't get a blast of cold air every time somebody came in or left. He was just taking the second bite of his sandwich and thinking is was better than his mother had ever made when a girl's voice suddenly broke into his thoughts

"Is this anybody's seat?" she asked politely, Tyler looked up to see where the voice had come from and was pleasantly surprised that the face looking down at him and smiling was rather beautiful.

"Err no, nobody's, please help yourself" and he motioned for her to sit, as she did so he glanced around the cafe and noticed there were several empty tables, *Simon* whispered quietly is his head, *you've pulled you jammy bastard !!!!*

Her name was Tina he discovered over the next hour or so, and after three coffees , also discovered that she too had left home and was renting a tiny bedsit in the town. She explained it was a dump but it was her dump which meant there was no aggro coming from irate parents if she smoked a cigarette, tobacco or otherwise, had a glass or two of cider or even the occasional blue pill. She told him Aldershot was a shit unfriendly place but that it suited her as nobody ever took any notice of her.

She told him her parents were very strict and were huge snobs. They had no idea how to bring up their only daughter, which is what she was. All they cared about was that she was home when they told her to be, didn't answer back and never moaned about being left to look after their three horrible dogs while they gadded off for weekends on their boat. Tina had a great sense of humour and Tyler was really enjoying her company. He bought them more coffee and then a bun each.

They talked and talked. They laughed and laughed and by five o'clock Tyler was lugging his backpack up the stairs to her room.

Tina, as it turned out was not quite the girl Tyler had first thought. During the evening and through the night he made more and more discoveries. She was a sex fiend was the first of these. Once they were inside her room she dragged him onto the bed and did things to him that he had only read about in some of his lad magazines. This was usually on the pages about "readers wives" when he had been in his bedroom, masturbating and dreaming that one day maybe he would find such a woman.

Well find such a woman he had and what a woman she was, even though she was only just eighteen! She made a mockery of the letters he had read on those pages. After an exhausting hour or three of pure sex and madness they were both lying naked on the floor and discussing what they would do if they were rich. This was the next surprise discovery; Tina was a thief and a blackmailer. She told him how she could easily manipulate men. How she would single out a married man in a pub or club, which she said was as easy as eating pie, give them the come on, get them to bed and then, all during their sex, would be taking pictures of them with a tiny hidden camera she had perched on top of a mirror on the opposite side of the room. As soon as they were finished she would drop into the conversation that she was only fifteen. Usually they believed her and were so frightened she would tell on them that they would cough up the fifty pounds she would ask for. If they didn't or if she was feeling really bad that day she would inform them of the camera, not tell them where it was but just explain that they would be hearing from her. At this, even the tough ones caved and paid up. Although she still kept all the films, for investment she said, just in case she fell on hard times. She said the secret was to only ask for small amounts as the guys were more likely to have that sort of cash on them. Tyler was amazed he had found such a good match for him. He declined to tell her about the horrendous stuff he had done in the past, just told her about the odd thieving.

They called themselves T and T and made plans to rip off as many punters and thieve as much as possible and then move on to another town and do it again and again until they had enough money to create some sort of good life for themselves.

Well dreams don't always come true but they had a great run and a lot of fun for about six years. By this time they had moved twelve times and were renting a really nice apartment in Southampton right on the waterfront. They each had a tidy sum in their own bank accounts, enough to keep them going for a while. Tyler had learned to control *Simon* for the past first few years but recently had begun to get urges again and *Simon* was waking up. This worked out really well for the unknowing Tina because Tyler was getting a bit fed up with her and *Simon* was beginning to push forward some ideas of what to do about it. As if fate had intervened it was around this time that she had come home and announced she was off. No bye or leave, just she was off. She didn't want anything from him which was a wise move on her part or things might have been very different. So that was it. Tyler was alone again, in a nice apartment with money in the bank and no woman getting in his way now that *Simon* was around again, he was feeling good.

A few days passed with Tyler kicking his heals wondering what he wanted to do next when his urge for some excitement came to the fore in the form of *Simon* completely waking up. Tyler took a back seat while *Simon* decided that the excitement was going to be in the shape of a murder. After all it had been ages, he had never been caught or even questioned about any of the killings he had done, he was clever, he was full of his own importance and Tyler was just going to sit back and let it all happen. His taste for blood was getting stronger. Ideas started to form and by the end of the day he was ready to go out on the prowl for his next victim.

He had decided that this time it was going to be a man. Girls were far too easy a prey. He would find a rent boy who was gagging for some fun, and fun he would give him. He had never raped a man before and he was quite excited at the prospect. After all, who was going to miss some runaway who got his kicks and money through touting his arse to any punter who was that way inclined. He could rid the world of the scum and have some fun into the bargain.

He had been to the rough end of the dock area with Tina on a few occasions when she was setting up punters to be rolled by them so he knew exactly where to find a poor sap, there were plenty. He just needed to pick the right one as some of them had friends looking out for them.

It didn't take long for him so spot his target. It was just on the brink of darkness and the boy was standing alone, leaning against a wall that had a very dim security light just above his head. He looked sad and for a nanosecond Tyler came forward and almost pulled *Simon* back but *Simon* was far too strong for him so Tyler again slipped into the background and basically went to sleep.

Simon looked around him; they were completely alone by the look of things, no friends of his victim lurking about that he could see. As *Simon* had walked towards the lad he had noticed a few derelict warehouses along the route, he thought one of these would make a perfect cover so knew straight away that the boy was waiting for a punter and knew exactly where they could go.

The boy lit a cigarette and glanced around for a few seconds before he noticed *Simon* walking slowly towards him. He began to smile; he had good teeth and quite a handsome face. He looked about seventeen or eighteen, not scrawny or malnourished. Maybe he had only just started this life *Simon* thought. He didn't look anything like the grubby ones *Simon* had seen so many times. Again Tyler started to wake up and started to protest very weakly but *Simon* just pushed him back into the back of his head, go back to sleep you moron, *Simon* told him. This is my ball game.

"After a bit of action?" the voice sounded older than the years of the mouth it came out of. *Simon* said nothing, just carried on walking slowly towards the lad "It's thirty quid and you have to use a condom or I can do a suck for fifteen, condom for that too of course". *Simon* smiled at the voice but said nothing. He carried on walking a few more paces by which time he was ten or so yards past the boy, "OK twenty five" the voice said, sounding a little more desperate than he had intended. It must be a quiet night, *Simon* thought to himself. He turned slowly towards the voice.

"Ten" is all he said.

They paced the few steps back to the empty warehouse and the boy led the way inside. Three steps or so in he turned to *Simon* and said "I want my money now before we do anything"

Simon started to reach for his inside pocket, but before he had a chance to see what was before him a huge fist came from nowhere straight into his face. For a second *Simon* was stunned and started to wobble as his knees buckled under the weight of the blow, but he was having none of it and rallied fast, lashing out at his assailant with such force and using the hammer he had pulled out from his inside pocket. The body behind the fist went crashing down before him hitting its head as it fell and just lay motionless with just a trickle of blood oozing from the corner of its mouth.

"You've killer her!" the voice of the young lad screamed at him as he crouched down next to the still body of a rather huge girl. "You must go and call for an ambulance, she's not breathing!, I'm sure she's not breathing!" he was getting hysterical so *Simon* had to silence him with a blow. The boy's screaming stopped immediately when he realised just what *Simon* was capable of and started to sob quietly, rocking backwards and forwards and stroking the huge woman's head as he did so. Tyler woke and wanted to leave but *Simon* stopped him.

Isn't this just what you wanted? *Simon* in his head asked him, but even better now you have two. Tyler was gone now and *Simon* had total charge again. He pulled the boy off the woman and dragged him to the side where he pushed him roughly onto the hard concrete floor.

“Now you little shit” he said “Did you think you were going to rob me then, you and your friend?” and he motioned his head towards the lump of unmoving body lying by the door.

“I’m real sorry mate” the boy braved to speak “It was her idea; she said I just needed to lure a punter into here and she would do the rest. I ain’t never done this before, honest, and I’ll never do it again, but please get an ambulance for her”. The pleading look in his eyes made Tyler come back but only for a brief second. *Simon* was in charge now and no amount of pleading by the lad was going to change that.

“Yeah, well you won’t be doing it any more will you”, and with that he lifted the hammer and smashed it down as hard as he could onto the boys skull. The sound of the cracking bone made *Simon* smile, one of his beautiful smiles but this time so full of evil.

Leaning over the body he could tell instantly that the lad was dead so he carried out his plan. He donned his surgical gloves and slipped on a condom and proceeded to have anal sex with the still warm body. After he had satisfied himself he left the boy face down and naked from the waist down. He then walked over to the heap of what was once a woman, but was now very dead. He dragged her over to where the lad lay and piling her on top of him removed her clothing from the waist down too. He had no intention of doing anything with her, he was satisfied for the time being, quite elated after his first sexual encounter with a boy. He was very pleased with himself. Two killings, a real bonus one after all, he was only expecting to do one.

He walked to the door and peeped out to check if all was clear, when he was sure he left the warehouse, throwing the hammer into the harbour as he went and smiling to himself.

His elation as usual had dwindled by the time he got back to his flat. He was Tyler again, *Simon* had fallen asleep in the back of his brain and Tyler’s regret started to come to the fore again. He poured himself a large glass of whiskey.

He had taken to drinking whiskey whilst with Tina, originally to impress her but now the taste had got a hold on him and he really enjoyed the burning sensation his throat got when he swallowed it. But before he could drink the pure liquid he would need to shower and put on some fresh clothes. A drink such as good malt deserved such an honour.

Once clean and shaven he placed all the clothes he had worn that night into a bin liner, double bagged them ready to take them to some unsuspecting wheelie bin somewhere in the city. Probably at the back of some restaurant or cafe, where there would be a deposit of mouldy food or rotting fruit, a place where it was very unlikely to be foraged by anybody due to the awful smell once the lid was opened. He would take it the next morning though because for now he was going to sit enjoying his whiskey and formulate a new plan.

He had decided while he was in the shower that *Simon* was going to stay asleep now. He had wrestled with this demon for so long now and the small amount of goodness left in his fuddled brain, in the shape of Tyler was trying really strongly to come to the fore again. He had suddenly realised he was no longer yearning for more action. The disgust he felt in his "Tyler mind" of his last "event" had sickened him. When he had looked through Tyler's eyes at the huge dead half naked body of the woman that *Simon* had killed, and the pathetic boy lying under her, with his skull smashed in, his stomach had turned.

He was going to be a normal person. He had decided he was going to be stronger than *Simon,* this time he was going to win. At these calming thoughts, sitting in his comfortable chair, he drifted off into a beautiful sleep where he dreamed of being a family man with a wife and children. Children who he would love and cherish. A life so unlike the first part of his life where his birth mother didn't even know what day it was, let alone if she had any food in the house to feed him with, where her only real goal in life was getting to the next fix. Probably the best thing for him had been her overdosing and him being adopted.

His adoptive parents hadn't been so bad really, they were kind people but the damage had been done to Tyler by the time he was four or five, he had learned to despise adults. He hated to be told what to do and hence *Simon* had been born in his brain, as a protector. To keep him safe when his birth mother's so called boyfriends wanted to keep him quiet while they shagged or fixed up together, when he had been shut in the cupboard or gagged in his bedroom and then the door locked, when he had been beaten by them for asking for some food or a drink of water, and on the really bad occasions when they wanted him for sex. There had been many times when he had been passed around from one disgusting man to another all while his mother had been out of her head and hadn't even noticed the actions or listened to the screaming and sobbing afterwards. She had never noticed, or chose not to notice, the bruises on his arms and inside his legs. His poor body had been through so much torture. *Simon* had got him through all this. There was no wonder he had become such an important feature in his life.

It was amazing just how often the social workers had visited and never noticed anything wrong. His mother would always say what a good boy he was and, as he was always clean, even if a little shabby they assumed he was fine. He never seemed too thin as his mother always had him in bulky jumpers too big for him so no reports were ever filed against his home life. He had, on a couple of occasions tried to tell the social workers that he was abused, but his mother always convinced them that he was really good at making up stories. Then after they had gone she would cuddle him and tell him not to say such things, and that she loved him. That if he told stories like that they might just put her away and take him into a home. Six year old Tyler fell for this every time. He stopped bothering to say anything in the end as by the time he was eight *Simon* was devising a plan to get him out of such a life.

Then one day, after being locked in his bedroom for what seemed like hours, he heard his mother shouting for somebody to stop, then a bang, a door slam and then silence. He had cowered under the few skanky covers on his bed, with a gag around his mouth, peeing and fouling the bed for two days until he heard the sound of a door being bashed in and some voices, although he couldn't make out what they were saying, and then his bedroom door being broken open. An awful smell hit him as somebody gently lifted the covers from his head and a kind voice called, "He's OK , he's here." Suddenly there were people everywhere. He was lifted from the bed and wrapped in a proper blanket, the foul smell was still there, some of it him but most of it was, as he found out later, his mothers decaying corpse.

Apparently she had been with one of her "boyfriends" in the lounge when they had a fight about money, he had hit her (after she had hit him first was his story later) and she had banged her head on the corner of the coffee table, well that was his story. He had told the police that when he had left her she was still breathing. When they did the post mortem they discovered so much heroin in her body it would have killed half a platoon of soldiers. Of course they could never prove the "boyfriend" had administered it as she was a known junkie anyway so he got off lightly as all they could charge him with was with failing to call an ambulance after causing an injury.

Once Tyler was cleaned up and fed and supposedly sorted after such a trauma he had been fostered for a short time and then adopted by a god-fearing family who felt sorry for him and thought they could make a difference to his life. Tyler was nine, *Simon* had been put on the back boiler but had re-appeared after one particular scolding from his father. Although for nothing really serious, in fact all his punishment had been was no sweets or television for a week, but *Simon* had come to the fore again, to be the protector and became stronger and stronger and started telling Tyler to do horrible things, but as Tyler was getting quite used to being fed, watered and clean he decided to put *Simon* back, no more now. And for that moment, and quite some time after, he had actually meant it.

CHAPTER 8

New Zealand

(3 Years after their wedding)

Toby sat in his parent's front room staring out of the window. His father was pacing up and down and his mother was trying to busy herself pouring tea from a china teapot into the matching bone china cups. With a slightly shaking hand she offered one of the cups to Toby who waved it away.

"Look" his father began, and taking his offered cup sat opposite Toby. "I know it is the hardest thing in the world for you to do but you must think of yourself now. You haven't worked for almost three years; there is nothing for you here other than us and Tilly. She has been in her "state" for three years now and there has been little, well not any really, improvement. You must get your life back on track. We will be here for her, we will go and visit, and we will be her family, even though she doesn't know what is going on. She will never be ignored or left, we love her too son, but we love you and wasting your days hoping she will improve is not......." But before he could continue Toby stood up and shouted at his father

"You don't understand do you, none of you. She is my wife, for better or worse. I made a promise to her and I will stick by it. I have no life without her; I don't want a life without her. I want my Tilly back and one day I mean to get her. If I have to sit by her bed and talk rubbish to her each and every day I will bring her back".

"Of course that is very commendable" his father started again but a look from his wife told him to stop.

"Come and sit down" she told Toby. "Have some tea and we will speak no more about it."

"Bloody typical" Toby said but he did sit back down, cup of tea to cure everything, how typically English and here we are in bloody New Zealand. At this remark he softened his angry face and almost smiled at his parents. After all they were only trying to make him see their sense of it even if he didn't agree.

"I'll tell you what" he started "I will ask the doctor to have a chat with me again and if, and I mean only if, he says it will make no difference if I go back to England for a few weeks then I might consider going, but not to start a new life, just to see if I can get back into the police force and if so, if I can find a special hospital for Tilly assuming they say she is fit enough to travel of course."

Well it wasn't quite what his parents wanted to hear, but it was a start. They had asked him to come to discuss just what his plans were for the future. Currently he spent his days mooning around his tiny flat and then going to see Tilly for hours and then finally ending up in a bar and drinking until it was time to get to bed.

After his outburst at his parents' house Toby felt bad. He knew they only meant well and had his best interest at heart but he had left under a cloud, or felt he had anyway. Although they had all made up before he left he knew that they really wanted him to go back to the UK and continue with his life but he felt Tilly still needed him and he had no intention of deserting her now.

He walked to his local bar once he had taken his car home and was sitting alone in a booth with a glass of beer and a double vodka chaser feeling sorry for the row with his parents but also feeling that they were so wrong.

"Hi mate!" A voice broke into his thoughts "What are you doing here; I thought you were in the UK?"

Toby looked up not recognising the voice at first but as soon as he saw he face smiling down on him his heart soared.

"Bloody hell Daniel, how on earth did you find me?" Sit, sit, oh my god sit please!"

Daniel sat opposite Toby in the booth and explained that he had been in Thailand for the past four years and had no idea Toby was in New Zealand until he bumped into Toby's parents in the local market about two hours ago. They had said that Toby was around and could do with seeing his old school mate. They said he might find him in a bar close to home and "Well this was the closest and the first one I tried, bit of luck eh mate?"

Toby smiled, he hadn't seen or heard from Daniel for years, hadn't even known how to contact him as he knew he was travelling all over the world with the company he worked for.

"So Thailand eh, any Thai brides around then Dan?" Toby joked and for a short time it made him feel better.

They talked through four or five beers and then went back to Toby's for a night cap. Daniel wanted to hear everything that Toby had been up to in the years since they had last seen each other, and Toby wanted to hear the same from his pal. Daniel was really upset when he heard of all the events of Toby and Tilly's marriage, and of the horrendous events that led up to the situation they were in today. Daniel, on the other hand, had loads of fun stories which lifted Toby's spirits no end. They talked into the small hours, ending up with Daniel flopped asleep on the sofa and Toby, after throwing a blanket over him, retiring to bed himself.

Next morning they were both a little delicate to say the least, Daniel, picking up the now empty vodka bottle was shuddering at the thought of the past evening but after several cups of coffee and a huge amount of toast they both felt a little more normal. Daniel had expressed a wish to go with Toby to the nursing home where Tilly was so they headed off together.

They sat with her for just over an hour with no recognition from her when Daniel stood and indicated for Toby to follow him. Once out of the building he took Toby's arm and headed him towards a bench in the grounds of the home. They sat down, both had tears in their eyes but neither spoke for a few moments until Daniel broke the silence.

"Look mate I have to be honest here, I really can't imagine just what you are going through but I can see things from an outsiders point of view, You have to let go mate, you have to get on with your life. Would she really want you to sit by her bed every day just hoping that she will recover when the doctors have told you there is little or no chance that she will come back? She had no idea you were there just now." The tears that were moistening Toby's eyes a few moments ago were now pouring down his cheeks and a loud sob erupted from his throat and his body gave a huge shudder.

"I can't Dan, I really can't!" Toby was sobbing uncontrollably now.

Daniel placed a gentle hand on his mate's shoulder but said nothing until he had stopped shaking.

A few minutes passed before Toby calmed down and then suddenly something seemed to click in his brain.

"Of course!" he said looking at his friend. "I know exactly what I must do!" and with that he jumped up, patted Daniel on the shoulder and continued "I'll give you a shout later" and with those words he was gone, leaving Daniel sitting there totally bewildered. He watched as Toby headed back into the building. He wasn't sure what to do as they had both come in Toby's car which he had obviously forgotten about . Should he wait or follow him or what. He decided he would just go and wait by his car, he wasn't sure just what was going on in Toby's head at this time but he hoped it wasn't something bad!

His fears were unfounded as when Toby appeared almost an hour later he had a smile on his face and looked as if a massive weight had lifted from his shoulders.

"Arrh mate, I'm sorry to keep you waiting out here, I was just carried away with my plan!"

Dan looked at him puzzled "Plan?" he asked.

"Yeah I'll tell you all about it in a mo, let's go and get a beer and I will explain all".

Once seated with a beer in front of each of them Toby spilled out his plan.

"It hit me like a brick when we were talking on the bench earlier" Toby offered. "I was thinking that all I am doing is sitting with my beloved Tilly and not actually doing anything pro active to help her" At this Daniel tried to interrupt but Toby shushed him and continued. "Well I thought, what had made her be like that in the first place? Well part of it was because she found out that the bastard that did all those terrible things to her was still out there, somewhere on the loose. Well of course what I must do to help her is get him. Find him and make sure he gets what he deserves and only then can I come back to Tilly and tell her. I am convinced if I tell her hand on heart that he is no longer around I will get through to her and pull her back into our life". He then took a huge gulp of his beer, leaned back on his chair and told Daniel that he was going to rent out his flat and head back to the UK and find *Simon.* "The doctor thought it was worth a stab anyway" he finished with.

Daniel thought for a moment and then patted Toby on the shoulder and said "Good for you mate, I think that is the right thing to do." Although in his head he was thinking it was a total waste of time for so many reasons but if it got Toby back into the land of the living it would a good thing.

Toby's parents were overjoyed that he was heading back to England even though they were of the same opinion as Daniel regarding his aim, but humoured and encouraged him. They promised that they would continue to visit Tilly and would let him know immediately if there was any change, or even the tiniest hint of a change in her condition, good or bad.

Toby found a tenant for his flat without any problem and was ready to travel within three weeks of his decision. He had sent several letters to the police forces around the country to see if there was any chance of him returning to his previous position giving a reply address of an ex colleague that he had arranged to stay with for a few weeks until he got himself sorted.

He spent his last day in New Zealand sitting next to Tilly's bed, holding her hand and telling her of his plans. He explained that he wasn't leaving her, he would be back with the best news and that he would love her forever. At this point he almost had a change of heart and as the tears flowed down his cheeks he decided he would stay, but then the doctor walked in and seeing him distressed smiled, shook his hand and told him he was doing the right thing. Jolted out of his sadness Toby kissed Tilly for the last time and left her room. Wondering, and not for the first time, if he would ever see her smile again.

CHAPTER 9

When Tyler woke up the next morning next to his wife he felt good. He had decided he was going to ensure *Simon* was not going to spoil his life any longer. He had got away with his evilness for years due to his cunning but more probably a lot of luck. His handsome and innocent face had worked its magic on several occasions. He should really be languishing in a high security jail where they have thrown away the key, but here he was, next to his beautiful wife. Yes this is definitely what I want now he thought to himself, no more horrors of *Simon* making me do evil things. Today is now my new life, *Simon* is gone forever. I love this woman next to me; I will do right by her, no more fucking around and definitely no more violence. No, this is good, this is my new life.

Then the baby started to cry !!!!!

Sam stirred as the baby's sound worked its way into her maternal senses. She opened her eyes to see her husband staring down at her. She smiled and reached out to touch his face, the handsome face she had fallen in love with over and over again. No matter how he treated her she always forgave him in her heart. Making excuses for his irrational and bullying behaviour. All he had to do was kiss her and say sorry and she would forgive him anything. Her hand was almost touching his skin when he suddenly pushed her back and jumped out of bed.

"Enough!" he shouted at her shocked face, "Go and shut that bloody kid up, for Christ's sake!" and with that he charged out of the room. Sam looked stunned for a second but then knowing Tyler the way she did she said nothing , just pulled herself out of the bed and into a robe and started to head for the bedroom door. Dylan was screaming his head off by this time and Sam was getting anxious in case Tyler got even madder and took it out on him, but before she could reach the door the screaming suddenly stopped.

Sam rushed, although very quietly to the baby's room, almost frightened as to what she might see but not believing she should be worried even though she was, and there he was, Tyler, with Dylan in his arms cooing and gently rocking the child. Sam had never seen him behave like this before and tears welled up in her eyes. Tyler turned and gave her the special smile she hadn't seen in a long time and then holding his hand out for her to take pulled her gently to him and Dylan. He kissed her head softly and whispered that he loved her and was sorry for everything. "I will make it up to you now I promise" he said "We will be a wonderful family, maybe even have a little brother of sister for Dylan in time, maybe even two or three. At this they both started to laugh and Dylan joined in, of course he had no idea what he was laughing at but he could sense the calmness and happiness his parents we enjoying.

Once Sam had gone down to the kitchen with Dylan to feed him and get them all some breakfast Tyler stood in front of the mirror and talked to *Simon.*

"OK, so you tried to appear just now, you bastard, but I knocked you back didn't I? See I can do it, I am stronger now and I am going to be happy! I am going to have a normal family life, do you hear me? You are gone, gone, gone forever!"

"Is everything OK?" Sam called from downstairs "I thought I heard raised voices?"

"Nah sweetheart" he replied "just talking to myself, everything is just fine" but in the back of his mind he was saying please let it be.

They had a wonderful day out, just the three of them. Tyler was attentive and fun. They laughed together more in that one day than they had in their whole relationship. For the first few hours Sam was on tenterhooks, waiting for Tyler to explode into one of his terrible moods but he didn't. He was like a new person. She had never experienced him being like this for so long before. By the end of the day she actually dared to think he really had changed and that life was going to get better at last. She did think that maybe he had been seeing a counsellor or psychiatrist as the change in him was so drastic but she didn't give a shit. She had her man and he was being nice and she loved him so very much.

After Dylan was in his cot and sound asleep that evening Tyler took Sam's hand and led her upstairs to their bedroom where he made the gentlest love to her that she had ever experienced and after they lay in each other's arms making plans for the future. Tyler told her that he would find a better job, although she had no idea that he didn't actually have any job, he just robbed people. He said that the very next day he would go out and search and then together they fell into a beautiful and contented sleep.

The unbelievable happened the next day. Tyler got up, showered, dressed in smart clothes, changed Dylan, made coffee and carrying Dylan and a mug of coffee woke Sam up with a gentle nudge. She was so happy to see him leaning over her with Dylan in his arms she could have cried.

After he had left in search of his new career Sam called her mother.

"Honestly mum", she said "you won't believe the change in him, he is really trying and I am so happy." Her mother was pleased for her daughter but very sceptical, does a leopard change its spots so quickly she wondered. But just told her daughter how glad she was that things were working out at last and even suggested they go around for lunch on the following Sunday.

Sunday arrived and Sam's mum was nervous all morning preparing the lunch. She so wanted everything her daughter had told her about the change in Tyler to be true but she had seen for herself on many occasions the sadness in her daughter's eyes after one of Tyler's "episodes". She had seen her daughter try and hide the tears from her if she dropped in on her unannounced and asked where Tyler was? She had waited for the knock on her door to come at any time of the day or night to see Sam with Dylan in her arms saying she had left him for good. But this had never happened, Sam always defended him saying he was away on business and had forgotten to phone to tell her he had been held up, or that he was away with his friends for a boy's weekend. But Sam's mum knew a cover up story when she heard it. Still today was the day when she would be able to see for herself if in fact Sam was right and Tyler was a changed man. Her doubts far exceeded her beliefs, which is probably why she was so nervous and dropped a full pan of boiling potatoes on the floor in the kitchen causing Sam's dad to come rushing in from the garden to see what all the screaming was about.

Luckily there was no harm done, no burns or scolds just a wet floor swimming in partly cooked potatoes. Ten minutes later a fresh batch was boiling away, Sam's mum was sitting with a glass of wine and a friendly arm on her shoulder from her husband.

The lunch turned out to be perfect. Not only was Tyler behaving like the perfect gentleman, he was actually good company. Relating fun stories of when he was a boy, about how he had such a good upbringing with his four brothers and a sister. Then he made them laugh with his impressions of his mother catching the six of them hiding under the kitchen table after stealing her freshly made scones, and how she forgave them as she laughed while wiping off their jammy faces from eating them all. Every so often he would find Sam's hand and give it a quick squeeze and then turn to Dylan and gently kissed his tiny head. He told them how wonderful it was living in such a happy environment with such wonderful parents. How much he loved school and how his parents wanted him to become doctor which was totally his intention until his father had died suddenly from a heart attack leaving his mother alone, and then she got ill so he had put his dreams on hold to stay with her and help her look after his siblings. All this of course was total nonsense but as he was inventing his ideal family, he was starting to almost believe it himself. He was really enjoying inventing such a beautiful past and just couldn't stop once he had started. Even at one point showing tears in his eyes as he told them how he had held his mother's hand as she quietly slipped out of his life and up to heaven. Sam was in tears, her mum fighting them off and her dad stood and patted his shoulder telling him just was a wonderful son he had been.

Tyler was enjoying his new re birth. He hadn't had any movement from *Simon* for weeks now and had almost forgotten his existence.

Weeks turned into months and Sam started mentioning maybe they should have another baby. After all Tyler was doing well at the job he had managed to blag his way into. He had started at just taking orders for car repairs at the little garage not far from where they lived but as the business had grown suddenly he had been moved up to manager of the parts and bodyworks. He was loving it too.

When he got to work the next day Tyler started to reflect on things. After such a horrendous few years with *Simon* taking control of his life and all the terrible things he had made him do, Tyler was now a new man. He was content with his lot. He no longer went out thieving and screwing every girl who would let him. He had an attractive, if not beautiful wife, a wonderful son, a job, a place to live. What was not to be happy about? Yes, he thought to himself, yes maybe we should have a second baby.

When he got home that night carrying a bunch of flowers for Sam he suggested that after Dylan had gone to bed they order a take-a-way, have a glass or two of wine and make another baby. Sam was over the moon at this and Dylan was in bed twenty minutes earlier than usual!

Sam had got used to Tyler being gentle now with his love making, she enjoyed it much more than when they had first got together when he was rough and only content to satisfy himself so when he was more like his old self this night she was surprised. Just a rough "bonk" then he turned to go to sleep.

Now Sam's courage had grown immensely since the change had occurred in Tyler's behaviour so she had no problem in challenging him as to his rough and selfishness now, especially as they were trying to conceive a baby out of it. At first she thought he was going to hit her as he sat up in bed with a face like thunder clenching his fist. She was frightened for the first time in months, but then his face softened and he took her hand gently and kissed it. Oh my darling I am so sorry, I don't know what came over me. I must be a bit drunk on love...or that wine we have just consumed. This made them both smile and with that he patted her stomach and said....come on little sperm, there are eggs just waiting for you in here...its baby time. Sam snuggled down again and within minutes was gently snoring. Tyler on the other hand was wide awake and left the bed to go to the bathroom, where he locked the door and stood in front of the mirror. NO NO NO he said to his reflection, *Simon* you are not going to wake up EVER so fuck the hell off and don't try that again.

For the next twelve months everything was rosy again. Sam didn't get pregnant straight away but on the ninth month it happened. She was so excited to show Tyler the pregnancy test result she had got earlier in the day. As soon as he walked in the door that evening she thrust it in front of him, he just stood there and looked, firstly at the plastic tester then at her then back at the tester, then slowly it dawned on him just what it was showing.

"We're pregnant!" he shouted, a great grin on his face. Then they were both jumping up and down with excitement. "Have you told Dylan yet?" he rushed to the lounge where Dylan was sorting out his plastic bricks. "Hey little man you're going to have a sister!"

"Or brother" Sam chimed in. Dylan of course just smiled and carried on building his brick tower. One happy family.

Maybe it was the excitement, maybe it was the jumping up and down or maybe it was just bad luck for Sam and Dylan but what Tyler or any of them did not know at this point was that *Simon* was beginning to stir. ....

CHAPTER 10

Toby's plane landed at Heathrow. All the passengers were jostling to get off first to get on their way to where ever they were heading to next but Toby just sat in his seat. His legs did not seem to want to move. As the last of the passengers exited the rear of the plane a pretty flight attendant leaned over him with a concerned look on her face.

"Is everything all right sir?" she was asking.

Toby looked up at her and his face said it all. Tears were flowing down his cheeks, he tried to speak but no words would come out. The poor flight attendant wasn't sure what to do for a moment but then she put a hand on his shoulder and gently said " Sir, if you would like me to assist you from the plane, maybe we can get a doctor to check you over."

Toby managed to snap out of his dream at her kind words and sort of smiled "No I am just fine thank you he said "I must have just been half asleep, I can get off now."

"Well if you are sure" she replied but she wasn't sure, she had never seen somebody who looked so very sad. She could tell it wasn't a dream, but heh it was none of her business.

Toby managed to drag himself and his hand luggage from the plane. "Pull yourself together man" he told himself.

The shock of actually landing back in the UK had suddenly hit him. The thought of his beloved Tilly lying alone in her hospital bed was all too much for him. He had to get control again. He was here for a reason and he was not going to return until the bastard who had done this to his beautiful Tilly had got his comeuppance. Either by his hand or the hand of the law. Although he hoped it would be by his hand as he was sure if he ever found him he would only get satisfaction if he killed him himself .

Feeling stronger after these thoughts he collected his cases and headed for the taxi rank outside the airport. He was just getting in a queue for one when he heard his name called out. Turning, he came face to face with Oliver, his friend from the force. "That was lucky" Oliver said "I wasn't sure which flight you would be on, I just guessed this it would be this one after Keith told me you were arriving today"

"Oh mate, am I pleased to see you!" Toby almost gushed. "I didn't even know Keith would have told you I was coming."

"Come on Toby, you didn't think your old mates would desert you did you? Now come on, the car is in the car park and if we hurry I won't have to pay for an extra hour!"

"Same old Oliver!" Toby laughed and with that Oliver patted him on the back and they headed off towards the car.

On the journey Oliver explained that once he had told his wife Helen that Toby was coming back to the UK she had insisted he stay with them until he sorted out exactly what he wanted to do. At this Toby almost got tearful again at such a kind thought but managed to control it. "Thanks mate" was all he could get out but Oliver knew what his friend had been through and knew to keep quiet when necessary.

They arrived at Oliver's house at 7.00pm and as soon as he had parked the car in the drive Helen was there hugging Toby almost before he got out of the car. "Hang on a mo Helen" Oliver was laughing "Let the man get out first!"

Helen had made a lovely dinner for them all and although Toby was actually knackered he couldn't refuse such a wonderful spread and once he started to tuck into the starter of smoked mackerel pate he realised just how hungry he had been. This was followed by an amazing rack of roast beef with all the trimmings and washed down with a very nice Merlot. They ended the meal with some cheese as none of them was able to eat any desert. Helen had laughed and said not to mind as they would have it the next day.

When Toby collapsed into the very comfortable spare bed they had made ready for him he actually felt content for the first time in, well he couldn't remember how long. He knew that tomorrow would be the start of his plan. Get a job, hopefully back with the police and then find the bastard and not only kill him but make him suffer beforehand. Oh yes he would make him suffer alright. For all he terrible things he had done. With this thought in his head and the wine and food in his belly he slept a wonderful peaceful sleep.

The next day was Sunday and so Oliver and Helen left Toby sleeping while they walked their two dogs, returning to find him in the kitchen making coffee. The sun was out and it was very warm for an October day so they decided to take the dogs and all walk to the pub for some lunch. Once they were settled at an outside table and had ordered their ploughman's and beers Helen and Oliver exchanged glanced, not unnoticed by Toby, prompting him to ask what was going on.

"OK" Oliver said. "I might have a bit of news for you."

"Oh go on Oliver" Helen urged "Just tell him!"

"Well" Oliver began "I have had a word with the chief constable and he told me that unless something has changed in your security background since you were last here he doesn't see why you shouldn't come back in your last position with the old team at the station in Guildford. Obviously there will be checks done but heh mate...welcome back!"

Toby sat for a moment dumbfounded then with a great grin on his face raised his beer glass and toasted them both. "I had no idea I had such good friends!" he said fighting away tears that had started to well up. "I won't let the team down" he continued, deep down thinking how now he could really begin to plan his revenge on *Simon*.

It didn't take long for Toby to get back into the ways of his old squad. He spent the first week in the main office of the CID catching up on any new equipment they had and all the cases they were dealing with. There was nothing anywhere about *Simon* even though he knew the case was still open. Toby wasn't stupid and knew that they had passed it through to the cold case department so he wouldn't be tempted to get involved, but in his mind of course it wasn't a cold case. He was going to find the bastard but for the time being he was going to play good cop and follow his colleagues with their current investigations.

He had been back in action for ten weeks when he got a call from an old friend who had transferred to a different town before Toby and Tilly had gone off to New Zealand. Phillip had been one of Toby's closest friend's years before but had distanced himself as did quite a few others when all the trouble happened. He had written to Toby after the news of Tilly's illness had filtered back to everyone but that was the extent of their contact for the past two years.

“Wow Phil!” Toby said, thrilled to hear from his old buddy, "How the hell are you, it’s so good to hear from you!” he was genuinely thrilled by the call.

“Hi Toby” Phil said a little tentatively. “Are we OK? I mean I am sorry I haven’t been in touch but”

“Let me stop you there” Toby butted in “I am delighted you called, you’ve made my day!”

Phil relaxed immediately and they chatted like old chums as if there had never been any distance between them. Within minutes they had arranged for Toby to go up and stay with Phil in Coventry for a weekend. Phil was dying for Toby to see his new house and his wife was looking forward to seeing him again too, or so he told Toby anyway. The date was set for two weeks time when they both had a free weekend and all of a sudden Toby began to feel slightly alive again. He had something, albeit small, to look forward to.

He kept his head down and worked hard on his cases for the two weeks making the time fly by, he even got a thumbs up from his boss to let him know how well he was doing. He had managed to nail a gang of youths who had been terrorising elderly people and breaking into their houses to steal anything that was worth more than a fiver. He had managed to trace a runaway school girl and persuaded her to return home. That one had been hard. He was so relieved it had a happy ending but obviously hurt because his own ending was far from happy. Still, when he saw the look on the girl’s mothers face it helped.

Toby drove up to Coventry after he had finished work on the arranged Friday night. He found himself singing along to the radio at one point, and then felt guilty for allowing himself to feel even slightly happy knowing that Tilly was still in the hospital bed not being happy, or even knowing what happiness was. He had been calling the hospital every day regardless of what time it was over there. Usually they were really polite but he did think they were getting a bit fed up with him calling so frequently as they had told him over and over again that there was no change, and if there was they would let him know immediately. He had promised to phone less but hadn't put that promise into action yet.

As he was driving he began to think about everything and decided he would be no good at carrying out his plan to find and destroy *Simon* if he was on edge and miserable all the time. He had to get back to normal, to be an ordinary copper and not let his obsession with hatred and misery consume him and take him away from his goal. He was going to do right by Tilly. He was going to go back to New Zealand when justice had been served and Tilly was going to get well and everything was going to be perfect. A dream? Well maybe or maybe not.

Once again he found himself singing along to the radio, his spirit temporary lifted.

Phil came out to meet him as soon as he heard his car pull into the drive.

"Wow mate, nice house!" Toby said getting out of his car, impressed by the look of everything. It was a really big detached house on a small development with a tidy front lawn with neat flower borders and tarmac drive. A huge double garage to one side with a double carport attached to the front of it.

"I think they must be paying you too much!"

"Ha ha!" Phil replied "why do you think we moved? Houses are so much cheaper up here, although we did have a little windfall from Suzie's grandfather which helped, I must admit. Come on in - Suzie is dying to see you!"

Toby collected his bag from the boot of his car, slung it over his shoulder and headed behind Phil through the huge front door in to the house.

Within a nano second a big black dog was at his feet, sniffing his legs and wagging a massive tail, closely followed but two tiny versions of Phil squealing with delight at seeing him, although they probably didn't actually remember who he was they had obviously been primed to shout "Hello uncle Toby!" as soon as he arrived. Toby smiled, dropped his bag and scooped the twins up into his arms.

"Well you two, have you been good boys" The twins nodded excessively. "Well then maybe uncle Toby might have a little something in his bag for you!"

They both wriggled to get down dying to see just what was in the bag. As Toby knelt down to open it Suzie appeared from the kitchen drying her hands on a tea towel. With a huge smile on her face she threw her arms around Toby's neck and kissed him on each cheek "It's wonderful to see you, come on into the kitchen, boys leave uncle Toby's bag alone!"

"No it's OK" Toby said "I have a little something for them in there" He didn't need to get it out as the boys had already ransacked his holdall and dragged out two "squeegee monsters" squealing with delight again. "What have you got there?" Toby said " They aren't for you, they're my toys!"

The boys looked at him for a second then both laughed knowing of course that he was joking. "Thank you uncle Toby!" they both chorused and then ran off into lounge with their spoils. Toby bent down and retrieved a bottle of Jack Daniels, handed it to Suzie, then closed his holdall and followed Suzie into the kitchen. Phil went to the cupboard and took out three glasses,

"Still drinking this old stuff then" Suzie said "I'm afraid I still have to have a little cola with mine". reaching into the fridge to grab a can of coke. Phil poured them all a drink and they sat at the kitchen table.

"This is a great house" Toby said looking a Suzie "I love the kitchen, but love the smell of whatever you have cooking in that oven even more, I'm starving!"

They all laughed. "Well you will have to wait a little longer, I have to bath the boys and put them to bed before we eat" Suzie said. "They insisted on waiting up to see you so I am afraid I'm running really late tonight"

"That is no problem" Phil said "Toby and I will bath the boys and read the story".

It took ages to bath the boys as they insisted on taking their squeegee toys in with them, which then lead to a water fight with Phil and Toby joining in. It was only when Suzie called up the stairs that dinner would be ready as soon as they were that they eventually got the boys to bed, so exhausted that it only took one story and they were out like angels.

The guys walked down the stairs laughing and for that moment Toby felt great.

All three settled at the kitchen table, a beautiful dinner of braised steak, roasted potatoes and about every other type of vegetable Toby could imagine sitting on plates in front of them. Suzie had opened a nice bottle of Rioja and had it breathing in the middle of the table. Phil poured them all a glass which they clinked together in a "cheers".

"Wow this is amazing!" Toby said tucking into the dinner "Thank you so much for inviting me, and those kids of yours....well what can I say, they are just great! Tilly and I were....." then his voice trailed off as thoughts of Tilly filled his head, the thoughts of the children they were hoping to have one day. Phil could see the tears beginning to form in his friends eyes as did Suzie who nodded gently to her husband to do something.

Phil stood and put a hand on Toby's shoulder, "I'm so sorry mate, I can't imagine what you were or rather are going through, but we are here for you, and you know that"

Toby half smiled, picked up his knife and fork again and began to eat. "Wonderful dinner Suzie" he said, then turning to Phil "Sit down mate, I'm fine, and yes I know you are here for me. It is just the odd moment it all gets to me, I'll be fine just as soon as I catch that bastard!"

Suzie shot Phil a look as if to say "what the !!!!!"

Once they had finished dinner and had each scoffed down a piece of Suzie's delicious lemon meringue pie she sent them into the lounge with a glass of Jack Daniels each and an order to stay there, as she was more than capable of filling the dish washer on her own.

Each man took a big chair and tilted their heads back and both going "Aaah" at the same time.

"So" Phil started with. "What's next for you mate, I mean are you staying in the UK or is it just a temporary visit"?

"I'm here Phil for one reason only. I mean to find the bastard who did this to Tilly and all the other people he has taken or ruined their lives. I am not going to rest until he has his come-uppence either by my hand or the hand of the law but by one way or another. Then and only then I am going to go back to New Zealand to my darling Tilly and tell her. I know what you are thinking, that I will never find him, the trail is cold, he has probably left the country. I have thought of all these things but you see Phil, I owe it to Tilly, she is lying in a hospital bed, she doesn't even know me. Her brain has shut down all because of that evil man. I need to do something, I need to avenge my darling, you do see that don't you?" Toby took a sip of his drink and closed his eyes. He was fully expecting his friend to say something like "You must be mad or stupid" of similar. After all the police had been searching for the bastard for almost three years now and hadn't come up with any leads whatsoever. The clever shite was too clever even for the best CID brains. But he hadn't reckoned on the hatred Toby felt for him, or so Toby told himself. He was going to find him somehow no matter how long it took.

After a pause of seconds Toby opened his eyes expecting to hear Phil's voice telling him exactly what he was sure he was going to say but instead Phil was just staring into space, totally silent until suddenly, taking a sip of his whiskey and then placing the glass on the coffee table in front of him turning to Toby he said "You won't find him Toby, not alone anyway, WE will find him together" and with that he picked up his glass and held it out to Toby ready to toast. Toby responded with his glass and with tears forming once again in his eyes smiled at his friend.

"I wish you were working in the old station where I am", Toby said. "I'm staying with Oliver and his family at the moment, remember Oliver Chisholm? We worked violent crime together before I left."

Phil nodded "Of course I do, he's a great cop, but as for me not being there I can still help from this end, you can feed me anything from any intelligence you get and I can work from this end too"

"Oh cheers mate that will be great!" Toby was touched by his friend's offer.

"I'm sorry I'm such a cry baby at the moment, it is just that since Tilly's breakdown..."

"Enough of that" Phil interrupted. "There is no shame in crying after what you have been through, anyway are you ready for a refill ?"

Toby smiled and held out his glass.

CHAPTER 11

When Sam was seven months pregnant she and Tyler started to search though all Dylan's things to see how much was suitable for their new baby. They had both decided they didn't want to know the sex of the child but when it came to the second scan and they were asked the question they both giggled and said yes they did want to know. As it turned out is was a girl so they decided to search through all Dylan's stuff and discard any boyish clothes. Tyler had never been so happy. All thoughts of *Simon* had disappeared from his head, with the exception of a fierce headache he had experienced on the day Sam had told him of the pregnancy. Once *Simon* was safely away it was like he was a different person. A real person, a happy family man with a lovely wife and a beautiful son. A safe, kind and adoring husband just like in the movies. *Simon* no longer entered his thoughts or tried to get into his happiness to dissolve it. He was a new man.

On the rare occasions Sam mentioned anything about his past he always managed to distract her by saying he didn't want to dwell on the past, just to think of the future. She had said she understood that he was sad about his parents dying but that she had loved it when he had opened up at her mother's house that time, making them all laugh at the things he and his siblings got up to as children. how she would love to hear more and maybe meet his brothers and sister sometime. In truth Tyler had forgotten exactly what he had told them that day and was frightened he might say something that didn't match so he just looked sad and Sam never pushed further as she was just so happy to have such a wonderful man who loved her. And love her he really did. Tyler anyway......*Simon* not the case.

Ever since the day he had found out Sam was pregnant, and the awful headache that had ensued Tyler had made a point of shutting that part of his brain off. He had learned to do this at an early age, especially on the nights his mother had shut him in his room while she entertained her so called "friends" all for the price of a fix or two. He hadn't realised that *Simon* was in his brain at this time but just that thoughts entered his head, bad thoughts and he needed to keep them shut away. Of course as he got older and *Simon* had started to infiltrate his brain there was no hiding him away. Tyler enjoyed being *Simon.* He enjoyed him like the drugs his mother had become so dependent on.

When he was running his reign of terror (*Simon's* name for it not his) he hadn't a care in the world. But Sam had changed all that and now he wanted no part of *Simon* ever again so he had reverted to his brain shutting trick. In fact he had done so well with it that he had now forgotten almost everything bad he had done.

Now with a new baby on the way and everything rosy Tyler couldn't control his happiness. On many occasions he would get in from work bearing gifts for both Sam and Dylan and a host of little fluffy toys for the new baby. Sam was so happy too. This was their life. When she was almost due to have the baby things began to change slightly but Sam was so happy she barely noticed, like the odd time when Tyler would go quiet and lock himself in the bathroom for maybe an hour. She barely noticed him go into the bathroom and shout at himself, she barely noticed the mood swings were beginning to come back. She was just too busy being happy!!!

Tyler had felt the first sign that *Simon* was beginning to wake up in the middle of the night a few weeks previously. He had tried to ignore the feeling and the dreadful headache that came with the knowledge but there was nothing he could do to stop it. Having been able to contain him for so long Tyler had at last thought he was free but *Simon* was too strong to let this happen.

It had been a long time since his last outing, a long time since his thirst for blood and evil had been sated. He kept plugging away at Tyler to release him, little by little he had started to break down Tyler's resistance. Pick pick pick, like a wood pecker on a tree. Pick pick pick, until eventually Tyler's headache had got so bad he had started to cave in to *Simon's* force.

Then all of a sudden one night he was free!!!

Sam woke suddenly to hear her husband in the bathroom shouting. She jumped out of bed and rushed to see what was wrong. She found Tyler lying on the floor holding his head and screaming "No, No, No!"

Sam leaned over him trying to calm him. She thought he must have fallen and hit his head or something but when she looked into his eyes she saw pure hatred, pure evil. Falling backwards with the shock of his face she hit her head on the side of the bath and shouted at Tyler to help her. He stood up and looked down at her with a look on his face that she had never seen before. It wasn't Tyler at all.

"Get up you stupid fucking cow!" he shouted at her but as she tried to lift herself up he just pushed her back down and started to kick her.

"The baby!" Sam screamed "Don't hurt the baby!" She had her hand over her swollen stomach trying to protect her unborn child but *Simon* was in total control now and he was more evil than he had ever been. His months of hibernation had made him hungrier than ever. With one final kick he left the room leaving Sam sobbing in a heap on the floor and Dylan crying in his cot, woken by the noise. Luckily *Simon* ignored the child and just grabbed at a load of his things, stuffed them into a holdall and left the flat, slamming the door as hard as he could behind him.

Very slowly Sam crawled to the door of the bathroom, she had violent pains inside her where he had kicked her and she was convinced the baby would be dead inside her. She just about managed to reach for her phone before the pain got so strong she almost passed out. She pressed her mother's icon and was so very grateful that her mother answered at once. "Mum, help!" was all she managed to get out before she screamed in pain.

It took only minutes for the ambulance to arrive, summoned by her mother immediately after she heard her daughter's voice. Luckily they were in the vicinity and so responded at once. Her mother had told them it was an emergency and that if the door was shut they must break it down. A little drastic from an hysterical woman they had thought and had considered their options should the door be shut but as luck would have it, in his haste to depart *Simon* had slammed the door so hard it had bounced back open which gave them an easy access. They found Sam lying on the hall floor, blood and liquid oozing from her and almost passing out with not only the pain but the horror and shock of what had just happened to her. Dylan was now screaming in his cot and totally inconsolable even when the lady paramedic tried to calm him. They were putting Sam on a stretcher having done everything they could to check her over and tested the baby's heart beat explaining to Sam that it was still strong. This helped to calm her a little. Then in true cavalry style her mother and father arrived. Picking up Dylan and settling him in her arms Sam's mum assured her daughter that everything was going to be fine. Although she had no idea whether it was!

"Where is Tyler?" she was asking. "We must let him know what is happening!" She had assumed Sam had been attacked by a burglar or something.

"It was Tyler!" Sam screeched. "He did this to me, he attacked me and tried to kill our baby!" and with that she let out another yell as a contraction came.

"We need to get her to the hospital as soon as possible" the Paramedic lady was saying. "You can follow in your car" and with that Sam was stretchered down to the waiting ambulance.

Simon was hiding around the corner watching the proceedings and waiting for the coast to become clear before he would be able to venture back inside the flat to collect anything he could take with him to sell or use. He watched as the paramedic pushed the gurney. Sam was covered almost completely over, which at first made *Simon* think that she might actually be dead but when he saw her mother reach out and stroke her head so he knew she was still alive, as if he cared he thought.

"Stupid bloody cow" he said to himself. "I should have finished her off."

There was absolutely no sign of Tyler left in his head now, *Simon* was in total control. He could see little Dylan snuggled against Natasha, Sam's mum's, shoulder. "I should have killed that little brat too" still no remorse, not a flicker of Tyler, he was long gone with very little chance of returning, so strong was *Simon* now.

The ambulance pulled away with Sam's parents about to follow behind in their car. Little Dylan was still snuggled in Natasha's arms as she got into the car. *Simon* crept around behind the bushes and let himself into the flat. He headed straight for the bedroom as he knew where there was some money stashed. Outside just as they were about to start the car Natasha realised that she was still cuddling Dylan

"Oh my goodness" she shrieked "We can't carry him like this, you had better go and find his car seat, I think I saw it in the hall way"

Roger switched off the engine and sighing got out of the car to go in search of the child's seat.

"Hurry up please Roger!" Natasha shouted to him as he raced back to the flat.

He didn't really notice that the door was ajar even though they had closed it when they had left with the paramedics, he didn't notice the shadow lurking behind the bedroom door, he just rushed into the flat with his head down in search of the car seat.

Whack, the back of his head felt like a hammer had fallen on it, well it had really, not quite a hammer but the heel of a boot, whack again, this second blow sent roger flat out on the floor face down almost unconscious. The third blow did render him out cold. *Simon* picked up the items he was taking which was the money from the bedroom drawer and some jewellery that Sam had been left by her grandmother and then giving Roger a final kick in his side left the flat.

Natasha was waiting by the car impatiently for her husband to return with the seat but after ten minutes she went back into the flat in search of him.

Simon was well away by this time so there was no sign of anybody around except her poor husband lying face down on the floor.

It was just like Groundhog Day as once again a team of paramedics were summoned and once again a gurney was wheeled out of the flat and into a waiting ambulance. This time Natasha, still clinging onto poor Dylan, climbed into the ambulance with her husband and, once belted in, held his cold hand all the way to the hospital. The paramedics had the siren going on the way which didn't instill a lot of confidence as to her husband's condition if they were in that much of a hurry, but they assured her that was necessary to clear the way and not a sign that her husband was dying. She wasn't sure if she believed them or not but it quietened her a little as she held even more tightly onto his hand and with her other hand held Dylan even tighter too .

As soon as they got to the hospital Natasha was told to go to the waiting room and that they would call her once they had assessed Roger's condition but Natasha was frantic not only for Roger but also for poor Sam who she had no idea where they had taken her.

She went to the inquiry desk and explained the situation albeit in an almost hysterical way but luckily the nurse in attendance was used to such and found Natasha a chair, settled her and Dylan and then, kneeling in front of her, calmed her enough so she could understand what she was actually trying to tell to her.

Within minutes of hearing her story the nurse had passed a message for her colleague to call for the police, she had managed to locate a junior nurse to take Dylan to the day nursery and to get him something to eat and was heading for the maternity suite with Natasha in tow. They arrived just as a doctor was coming out of one of the delivery rooms so the nurse grabbed him and explained what was going on and asked if he knew where Sam was. Pointing to a room a few metres down he smiled at Natasha's ashen face saying "It was a girl, a little small but mother and baby are just fine!"

The relief Natasha felt was beyond belief as she, with the nurse in tow, raced to the room the doctor had pointed to. Sam was laying back in the bed with her eyes closed, no baby in sight and for a second or two her mum thought the doctor had been wrong and the baby hadn't been born or was even dead, but just then a midwife walked into the room carrying Natasha's new granddaughter. Sam opened her eyes and smiled at the midwife before she noticed her mum was in tears standing beside her.

"Oh Mum" she wept too, "the baby is fine and I am almost fine. A few bruises that's all". Then as the tears started to roll down her cheeks she asked meekly "Have they caught him?"

Taking the baby from the midwife and nestling it in her arms she continued "Where's Dad?" then suddenly in a panic "where the hell is Dylan?"

Natasha pulled a chair up next to Sam's bed and smiled at the nurse, as if to say thank you so much, we are fine now. Then added very guiltily, almost as an afterthought as she had been so concerned with Sam "Please let me know as soon as possible about Roger"

"Of course" the nurse said and patted Natasha's shoulder then added "and the police will be here soon to take statements I'm sure"

At this statement Sam opened her eyes wide and "What police? I'm not going to press charges, Tyler didn't mean it, he just had a breakdown of something, he wouldn't normally have hurt us, something must have happened to him, I don't want any police!"

Natasha put her hand over Sam's and ever so quietly explained what had happened to Roger, and then as if the flood gate had opened she started to cry, huge sobs. "I don't even know if your dad is alive" then suddenly she was she was shouting "that bastard beat hell out of him, it's not only you Sam, he is evil and the police must catch him!"

Together Sam, Natasha and the new baby, arms around each other all cried.

Five minutes later the nurse came into the room carrying Dylan who was crying but stopped immediately he saw his mother and reached out his chubby little arms to her to hold him.

They held each other for what seemed like forever until Dylan started to squirm. Natasha broke free from the huddle and started to say she would go and see how Roger was but stopped when the doctor who was attending to Roger came into the room. Natasha could tell immediately from his expression that the news was going to be bad.

She watched, hardly daring to move or speak while the doctor pulled the door open a little wider and motioned for Natasha to follow him into the corridor. Doctor Willis was a kind and gentle man and hated having to tell any relative of bad news. He put a very light arm onto Natasha's shoulder and guided her into a relatives room a few yards down and once he had her seated very carefully and quietly explained that Roger had passed away a few minutes earlier. Apparently the blow to his head had caused a massive haemorrhage in his brain and there was no chance he could have survived, even if his heart had not stopped beating he would have been on life support but could never have recovered.

A nurse came in a few seconds later armed with a cup of tea which Natasha waved away. Why is it that the English think that a cup of tea will solve any problem she thought to herself, I have just been told my husband is dead and they think a cup of tea will make it all better? She knew she was thinking stupid thoughts but what else was she to think, her world, her safe lovely world had just collapsed before her eyes. What the hell was going on, what was she going to do? She stood up and walked over to the tiny window that overlooked a pretty garden, again she thought, obviously well planned out to calm grieving relatives, but she was not calm. Then she began to scream !!!!!

CHAPTER 12

News of the attack had spread and when the police arrived at Sam's flat there were people everywhere. There was blue police tape at the entrance but nosey neighbours were pushing through trying to see what all the fuss had been about. The constable trying to guard the entrance was 21 but looked about 12 and was having terrible trouble controlling them.

Toby and Oliver arrived and really annoyed as the crime scene was being totally contaminated but with a few politely stern but effective words easily got the crowd to disperse. Once inside they started to search for clues as to what the hell had actually happened A heavy work boot with a steel heel rim and coated in blood was discarded behind the door and was taken for forensic tests, also several items and a few child's toys so they could compare, what they assumed to be the weapon, prints or DNA to the inhabitants of the flat. They continued all the normal checks and then headed off to the hospital leaving the forensic experts to go through the flat with a fine tooth comb.

On their way to the hospital they were informed that it was now a murder enquiry as Roger had just died.

Oliver was going through the procedures as they were driving to the hospital but Toby had other thoughts on his mind. It was something that one of the neighbours had said as they were trying to disperse them at the scene. What was it now he thought, something about a guy that seemed to have some kind of split personality. How he had seemed really normal when they had first met but had changed in an instant. Had frightened Sam on a couple of occasions but that she had pooh -poohed it afterwards saying he had meant nothing by it. Toby started to piece a few thoughts together and it didn't take him long to decide that maybe just maybe he had found *Simon* !!!

Once at the hospital Oliver went off to interview Sam while Toby went to try and speak with Natasha. He found her in the relatives room with a nurse, a box of tissues and a cup of untouched tea.

He quietly entered but Natasha didn't look up, just head down with a handful of tissues against her face. The nurse consoling her looked up and motioned for Toby to sit near them and then with a very genteel voice tried to coax Natasha to look up.

"Hello" Toby said as gently as possible "I know, well I don't know but I am trying to imagine just how awful this is for you at this moment but I must ask you a few questions. We need to get the bast... I mean person who did this as soon as possible. Now I know it is totally the wrong time to be asking questions but we do need to sort this as soon as possible before he has a chance to get away."

Natasha looked up, tears streaming down her face but she looked in control. "It's OK" she turned to the nurse and said "you can go now, I'll be OK" the nurse looked at Toby and he nodded so she left.

"I'll be back in a little while" she said and closing the door behind her mouthed to Toby "Please be kind"

Toby moved close to Natasha and taking out his notebook proceeded to ask her to explain the chain of events, which she did bravely. She liked Toby instantly and although was heartbroken at the attack on her daughter and the horrendous murder of her husband she found the strength to tell Toby everything she knew. "Please get him" she said "don't let him destroy another family. Get him and lock him away forever"

"We will do our best" Toby said." I can promise you that!"

"I believe you" Natasha said and with that the nurse came back in and Toby left her to take control again.

Oliver and Toby met in the canteen of the hospital grabbing a coffee and comparing notes before they returned to the station. "You think it's him don't you?" Oliver said "I could see the look on your face when that neighbour was talking, but don't jump to soon, not until we have a few more witness statements, you may be wrong and it could mar your judgement"

Toby gave him a "look" that said it all. "It's him" was all has said.

Once back at the station Toby wasted no time in plotting in his mind his next move. He would wait for the witness statements to be collated and then discuss the next move with Oliver, that was plan B, plan A was that he would find this bastard and watch him as he dies a slow painful death, the cause of which Toby had yet to plan. But just the thought of it brought an almost smile to Toby's lips. You are still out there, you are close and I will get you, was all that was in his mind.

Oliver arrived at his desk twenty minutes later with a flat white and a bran muffin. Hi mate, here you go. Statements are beginning to come in now so we can get started in a few minutes. Toby nodded and took the coffee but brushed the muffin away and patted his stomach. Oliver just smiled and withdrew the muffin saying he was glad and proceeded to take a huge bite from the treat.

Ten minutes later they sat hunched over Toby's computer screen downloading the statements as they were loaded from the phones of the PC's interviewing the witnesses.

The descriptions coming through were very similar, it was him !!!!! OK he was known as Tyler to Sam but the photo they had managed to find. It was at their wedding and had been torn into four pieces. Sam had explained that Tyler had told her he never liked his photo taken but she had persuaded him to allow just one of their wedding. After three or four statements Oliver conceded, he looked at Toby, raised one eyebrow as if to say, OK so now what.

Suddenly Tina, one of the trainee girls from the outer office peeped around the office door and sheepishly clearing her throat first said "Excuse me, I am sorry to bother you, err but might I have a word please". Toby and Oliver looked up in surprise. Neither of them had ever really noticed let alone spoken with her before and the question on their faces was what the hell was so important that it disturbed two senior officers trying to solve an horrendous murder case. But they were two decent men of course and so they just side glanced one another and beckoned her inside.

"The thing is" she began in a voice they could hardly hear "I have this friend you see ..."

"Can you speak up please?" Oliver said trying not to show his minor irritation.

"Oh yes, sorry." She hung her head even lower.

"Come on now, sit down and say what you have to say sweetheart, I promise we won't bite"

With that Tina raised her head and with a little more confidence half smiled at the two men.

"Well, as I said, the thing is ..." Oliver suppressed his agitation again "I have this friend who has been seeing some guy for a few weeks now but I am very worried that he is not as he seems to be."

With this statement both men suddenly took more of an interest, mainly because it was close to what they had just been discussing but inside Toby had a sudden gut wrenching feeling that this might be important. "Go on" he urged "what makes you think he is not what he seems?"

Tina was quiet for a moment as she tried to get the words right, she didn't want it to come out all mumbled or they would just dismiss her worries.

"Well" she started again" my friend Orla met this guy in a club a few weeks ago, they went out on a few dates which seemed OK, she told me all about how charming he was and how kind and considerate, how he said he was very keen on her but he would never take her home to his house, he has never told her where he lived or anything really about him. They just used to go out and then back to her flat. Well at first she wasn't too worried but then when she started to feel a bit more serious about their relationship she began to worry that maybe he was married or living with someone. He had never volunteered any personal information about his current status or previous for that matter. She had decided that if they were getting serious she needed to know. She asked me to go along with her for a drink on one of the nights she was meeting him in a pub after work so I could meet him and maybe suss him out before she asked him these personal questions. Well I met him and he was charming as she said he would be but there was a bit of an edge to him. Anyway after an hour or so I left them in the pub and went to walk home. I got just around the corner at the end of the street when he suddenly appeared behind me and called my name, as I turned he grabbed me around the neck and pushed me against the wall. I was terrified, he told me to keep my nose out of his and Orla's business and that if I told Orla anything about him speaking to me I would regret it. Then he just pushed me to the ground and in a really bright and happy way just said "Take care now Tina and remember what I said" and he was gone."

Toby and Oliver looked at each other not knowing just what to think.

"What happened then?" Oliver asked "Did you report him to anyone?"

Tina shook her head, "I was too frightened to say anything for a couple of days but then I thought I owed it to Orla to tell her so I phoned her and asked if I could pop round after work for a coffee. I thought that if she didn't believe me or thought I was making it up because I was jealous or something it would be up to her to decide whether friendship was more important than being with a weirdo. Well I needn't have worried, she believed me straight away and it was obvious just why".

At this point the door of the office was pushed open with force and in came the duty sergeant

"Sorry to break this up guys but I have a lady downstairs who is desperate to see one of you and by the look of her she is not joking!"

Oliver jumped up and said he would go with the sergeant so Toby could continue with Tina.

Once the door was closed Toby turned to Tina and nodded for her to continue.

"She had two very black eyes and had obviously been crying for some time. I asked her what the hell had happened and she told me that *Simon*, the guy she had been seeing"

Toby jumped at this as it was the first time Tina had mentioned the name of the bloke involved in this mess. "*Simon* you say, his name was *Simon ?*"

"Oh I am sorry I didn't tell you that did I, well anyway she said that *Simon* had been around that morning and wanted to make love with her, she had explained that she had to go to work and he could come round later, thinking he was just being very romantic but he said she should take the day off. He was very persuasive so she agreed and phoned work to say she had a bad headache" at this statement Tina gave a sarcastic grunt as if to say that was almost ironic. "Anyway apparently they went to bed but he was being very rough so she asked him to stop which he did grudgingly, I am sorry I feel very embarrassed for Orla telling you this but it is important, well he wasn't happy but stayed cuddling her. Then she asked him if he was serious about their relationship and if so she would like to know more about his past and present circumstances. Apparently he just flipped. He leapt on top of her and forced his way into her, rape I would call it although she might not want to proceed with that accusation, well after he hit her in the stomach, pulled her off the bed and threw her face down on the floor smashing her face against the side of the chair. He then got dressed, kissed her on the top of her head as she lay there and went off saying he wouldn't be seeing her again giving her a horrible throaty laugh as he left" Tina looked up at Toby.

"Has she reported this yet" Toby asked.

"No she won't" Tina said "she is too embarrassed but she must, he is evil!"

Toby knew only too well just how evil *Simon* was, and now it seemed he had control again.

A few seconds later Oliver returned with a woman in tow, as she walked into the office. Tina jumped up and rushed over to her. "What has happened?" she asked. "Has anything happened to Orla?"

Orla's mum looked firstly at Toby and then at Tina "What are you doing here?"

The four of them settled around the small office. Toby sent Tina out to get them all a coffee and while she was gone had a chance to concentrate on what Orla's mum had to say.

She explained that her daughter had arrived at her house in a terrible state. She was bruised and bleeding and just collapsed into her mother's arms as she had opened the door for her. "It seems" she continued "that this guy she had been seeing had got a bit rough, a bit rough, she had challenged her, it looks like he has almost killed you!"

Both Toby and Oliver glanced at one another and Toby mouther to Oliver "His name was *Simon*". Oliver understood straight away and they knew exactly what *Simon* if it was in fact their *Simon*, was capable of and realised just how lucky Orla had been, but neither of them thought it a good idea to enlighten Orla's mum at this point.

Seconds later Tina came in carrying four polystyrene cups of steaming coffee on a tray. Putting is carefully on the desk she looked at Toby and asked if she should stay to which Toby gestured to the empty chair and Tina sat.

"OK" Toby opened "now can we go through this from the beginning, I want to know everything about this *Simon*, where he met Orla, how long she has known him, what sort of person you both thought he was, basically everything you can tell us". He looked at both ladies, "also I want you" and he motioned to Orla's mum "to allow me to send a police officer to your house to collect your daughter and bring her here so she can tell us her story.

Orla's mum looked surprised, "Don't you think we are telling you the truth then?" she asked, going red in the cheeks as anger was beginning to build up "Because if you think we are just making this up to spite this man *Simon* I can assure that we are most definitely are not!" She looked as if she was going to stand up and maybe even leave but Oliver put a gentle hand on her shoulder and very softly began to explain.

"I'm afraid we have to tell you something" at this point he glanced at Toby who gave him a very slight nod " You see, we do believe that this *Simon* is a person we have been trying to apprehend for some years now and if he is the same man then he is a very dangerous one and your daughter has been very lucky indeed." The gasps from both women were audible.

Orla's mum looked close to tears but pulled herself together before starting " Of course you must go and get Orla but I think I should go with the officer as I might need to persuade her." Toby nodded.

"I'll get a female officer to go and of course you can go too er Mrs, I'm sorry I don't know your name"

"Nicky, Nicky Adams, but please just call me Nicky, I am sorry I got cross earlier, if this man is the one you have been looking for and you say is dangerous, just what has he done ?"

"I'm sorry but I can't give you that information at the moment but I can promise you if it is him he really is extremely dangerous and the sooner we catch him and get him off the streets the better, I think Orla may be the one that can help us the most, we must know if he is the man we are looking for and if so we must track him down."

At this point a police woman knocked on the office door and entered saying she was ready to take Mrs Adams to collect her daughter.

They watched as Nicky left with the PC and looked at Tina, "Thank you for involving us in this Tina, you did the right thing, if it is OK we will let you know when Orla is here and you can join us when we interview her if you like, if fact we would really like you to as you are her friend and she might be happier with you there too."

Tina smiled a sheepish smile, delighted she had bothered to tell them all she knew and that she could hopefully help her friend and maybe even be a party to catching this horrible man. She left the office saying she would be around and just to give her a shout when they needed her.

As soon as she was out of the office Toby and Oliver looked at each other and almost smiling joined in a high five.

"This is it Oliver." Toby said "This is when we catch the bastard" !!!!!

CHAPTER 13

Simon was totally in control of Tyler's body now and he felt euphoric. He felt freer than he had ever felt, free to carry on exactly as he wished. The beast in him was no longer being suppressed by that idiot Tyler, he had no thoughts of his baby, no thoughts of the damage he had done to so many, all he could think of was that he was free.

He didn't look back on the devastation he had caused at Sam's flat, in fact he had almost forgotten exactly what had happened. He knew he had money, some clothes in a holdall that he had taken and the small amount of jewellery so his first stop was the cash converters shop in the high street. He only managed to get a small amount as the shop assistant looked a bit suspicious with his story of his mother dying and leaving him the ring, he had looked at her with his evil eyes and she had paid out fifty pounds to get him out of the shop. Still that was another fifty pounds he thought, should be enough to cover the train fare to Cardiff. He hadn't decided where he was heading until he overheard two girls discussing a hen night they were planning in Cardiff so he thought that might be as good place as any.

He went to the station and bought himself a ticket and sat waiting with a latté and an almond croissant on platform 3 waiting for the Cardiff train to arrive. He had only been there about five minutes and hadn't even begun to nibble on his croissant when a girl of about sixteen came and sat next to him. He glanced at her and realised she looked as if she had been crying, she still had a tissue in her hand and was dabbing at her eyes. She turned and saw him looking but he put on his best smile. Within ten minutes he had learned that she had just had a huge row with her father and she was heading to Swindon to stay with her married sister so she could calm down for a few days and put some space between her and her dad. *Simon* handed her his coffee and croissant and while she drank and ate he went and got himself another, thinking "this is just too easy".

They boarded the train together but before they reached Swindon *Simon* had persuaded her to go with him all the way to Cardiff. "Taking candy from a baby!" *Simon* thought. "Taking candy from a baby!" He felt so smug, if he could have patted himself on the back he would have done so.

Even though he had evil eyes he had a way of smiling that seemed to melt girl's hearts, so once he turned on the "*Simon* smile" they were putty in his hands. He took Rebecca, as he discovered she was called, for a fish and chip supper in the first cafe he could find in Cardiff. After all, he thought to himself, he didn't want to spend too much money on her as she wasn't going to be around for more than a short time, a very short time.

He made her laugh, he made her feel safe. After their fish and chips he took her to a busy pub where he thought they would just be one of the crowd, nobody would remember them. He bought her a bottle of WKD but just had a half of lager for himself. Being only sixteen he thought she would be tipsy after a couple but he hadn't reckoned on her being a modern sixteen year old who could certainly hold her drink. After the third one she was still sober so he decided he should add a little spice to her drink. He didn't want the barman to see him so he asked for a WKD for her and a double vodka and tonic for himself but to have the tonic left in the bottle separately. Once he was pushing his way back to their table he poured the vodka into her drink and the tonic into his glass. It still took two more trips to the bar to get her slurring her words and leaning on him and flirting. When she started getting a little too loud and friendly he decided it was probably time to leave as he didn't want anybody noticing them.

They went outside into the street which made Rebecca get very unsteady on her feet as the cold air hit her. She leaned onto *Simon* for support and he gently responded. "Putty in my hands" went through his head once again as he tightened his grip. As they had left the train earlier *Simon* had noticed a pathway to the side of the station which looked as though it led to a small wood. Perfect, he had thought, and now that was the direction they were heading. Rebecca started to giggle and hold on even tighter to *Simon.* "This is going to be so bloody easy" he thought to himself, "maybe too easy"

They giggled together and Rebecca staggered while *Simon* held on to her. If there were any passers-by they would look like any loved up couple heading for a bit of naughtiness in the woods. As it happened they only passed one man who was walking his dog, *Simon* had smiled at him and gave him a look as if to say "look at her, she's had a little too much but I am looking after her" as if you could give such a look. *Simon* could! The man had just shrugged slightly and half smiled back. "Not a problem there" *Simon* thought to himself, stupid bloody dog walker. They carried on walking until he found the perfect spot under some trees . It looked pretty secluded so well away from any prying eyes and even looked reasonably dry he thought, after all he didn't want to mess up his only decent trousers.

He took off his jacket and began to lay it down on the ground when he thought to himself, why get my jacket dirty, I'll use her coat, she won't be needing it again. At this thought he smirked to himself. "Take your coat off sweetheart" he said with the best smile he could muster on his face "Let's have a little lie down and a cuddle". Rebecca obliged and *Simon* took it from her and laid it on the grass. He pushed her, a little too rough for Rebecca's liking, but she obliged anyway.

Whether it was the way *Simon* appeared to be changing or the chill in the evening, Rebecca was beginning to sober up very quickly. She was beginning to feel a bit unsure of the situation too. *Simon* had been a real charmer on the train and really nice and friendly feeding her fish and chips and a few drinks in the pub but she was sure she had drunk more WKDs in the past than she had drunk tonight without feeling so woozy, and now he was becoming a bit strong and pushy. She was thinking that maybe she should say good night to him and get the next possible train home, make it up with her father and feel safe. As he pushed her further back and started to lean heavily on top of her she pressed the panic button in her head and cried for him to get off. The change in him was amazing, he stared down at her with his devil eyes, not the kind friendly ones he had used earlier.

"What the fuck are you shouting about your fucking whore, you can't lead me on and then say no, bloody well shut up!" and with that he punched her straight in the face making her scream even louder. He started pulling at her clothes tearing them as much as he could to get to her body. She started to scream again but his hand clamped over her mouth with such force she could hardly breathe. That's when she realised that she couldn't breathe and that was obviously what he wanted, he was going to kill her. *Simon* was on a roll now, he had his prey, she was almost naked and would stop breathing very soon, what a great night. He was just about to enter her, by now she had gone into a faint so he had removed his hand from her mouth, and now he thought, now I will be able to perform as I want to before I kill her. Nice to fuck a live one.

But he hadn't reckoned on the "stupid bloody dog walker"

Before he had even got his penis insider her a big Labrador dog appeared in his face, "what the fuck........" then a voice, "Here Petra, come here", then the stupid dog walkers face appeared staring down on him.

It took a nano second for *Simon* to get a grip and then a further nano second to leap to his feet and run, pulling up his trousers as he went but leaving his holdall behind.

The "stupid dog walker" who happened to be a really nice guy called Charley Tomkins bend down and pulled Rebecca's clothes down to cover her modesty thinking she was just out for the count because she was drunk but as he knelt down he realised she was hardly breathing. Grabbing for his mobile phone he dialled the emergency services and then, pushing Petra away from the poor girls face he started to apply mouth to mouth. Suddenly Rebecca started to breathe and opened her eyes and for a few seconds she thought she was being raped but then realised it wasn't *Simon* leaning over her although she wasn't sure just what was happening. She opened her eyes wider to try and focus but then fell back into the faint again. Charley was still trying to revive her when the paramedics arrived. He explained what had happened and let the paramedics take over, then the police arrived. Their first reaction was to arrest Charley thinking he had done something to the girl but once they let him explain and they saw Petra and the holdall that had been left behind they changed their view.

"We will need you to come to the station sir" Sergeant Wilson said, and give us a full statement and description of the man she was with"

An arrangement was made for Charley to take Petra home and then drive himself to the police station to give the necessary information.

At the hospital, as the paramedics had done such a good job in reviving Rebecca when the doctors examined her they were happy to transfer her to a ward just for the night to make sure there were no complications. The police had interviewed her and she had told them everything. The police asked the hospital if they would take a blood sample to check if Rebecca had been drugged, although the rape drug that seems to be what everyone is using nowadays doesn't stay in the system long enough to be traced. Rebecca had told them that she was convinced he was actually going to kill her and not just rape her. The police had contacted her father and he was on his way to see her.

When Charley arrived and gave his statement they asked him about the holdall. He had explained that when he had seen them staggering down the pathway he had noticed the holdall as it looked very full and was making *Simon* (or the man he had seen with Rebecca) wobble a bit with it on his back. He said he was a little concerned because of the look the man had given him, he wasn't sure what it was exactly but he thought he looked a bit evil. It was, after he had got halfway home he had decided to go back just to check everything was OK. The police explained that if he hadn't done that then they would probably be collecting a corpse from the wood rather than a live girl so they and of course Rebecca were very grateful for his instincts. They said she had asked if he would go and see her in the hospital if he had the time as she wanted to thank him herself.

The police opened the holdall but there was nothing in it to identify the man who had done this terrible thing, although there was a fair amount of money and some clothes which they sent off for testing for DNA. They did think though that unless he had a bank account and/or a card on him they were sure he would be looking to get some more money from somewhere locally so they put out a call to all cars to check out any strange local movement, especially small shops or garages where easy access to money is possible. There was no reason for them to think this was anything but a chance encounter in finding Rebecca but obviously a very dangerous man if Rebecca's tale was to be believed, although they did think that maybe he was just very rough and wasn't in fact going to actually kill her. The jury was out on that one at this time.

Simon kept running and didn't look back until he was at the station and sitting in the waiting room. It was then he realised he had left his holdall behind. Rage erupted inside him and he was so furious, not as you might think with himself, but with Rebecca. He put all the blame on her, of course it was all her fault, stupid bitch. If she had stayed quiet he could have shagged her and then smothered her and gone on his merry way. Well he has now learned that maybe not everything goes his way so he will have to be a bit more careful. Now what was he going to do about money then. OK he has a fifty pound note in his shoe, something he has always done whenever he's had a fifty that he could afford to stash that is. So he thought for a minute or so and then decided the best plan was to get another train ticket to somewhere else, miles away as soon as possible. Then, hearing a police siren going in the distance he decided that that time was now.

It was 9.00pm and the ticket office was closed so he had no choice but to get on the next available train and hopefully pay on board or better still get a free ride.

Half an hour later a train came into the station. Only two passengers got off, one was a teenage girl and the other was an old man. As he rushed through the platform he bumped into *Simon* nearly knocking him over. He grabbed at the man and shouted

"What the bloody hell.....where's the fire?", at the same time sussing out as to whether he could pick his pocket.

"I'm so sorry" the man said "It's just that my daughter has just been attacked and is in the hospital and I am rushing to see her" *Simon* knew at once who he was talking about and let the man loose saying

"Off you go then mate, good luck" but thinking "bastard, that must be Rebecca's dad".

He boarded the train, settled in a seat opposite the electronic board stating where the train was heading for next thinking that maybe just a station or two would be OK. He closed his eyes for a moment and must have drifted off for a short time because when he woke up he saw that the next station was almost at the end of the line and that he was deep into Wales. Not the ideal situation he thought for getting any cash, too many locals to deal with. He needed a big city so at the next station he got off and crossed the platform to get the next train back up into England. He didn't care where but it had to be where he could become invisible and somewhere he could get some cash.

The station he decided to alight from was Bristol, he had been lucky whilst on the train as no inspector had been on it and the barriers were almost deserted as it was very late when he arrived. He just jumped over one of them and headed straight for the exit. Unfortunately he was not alone and a station guard spotted him and shouted for him to stop but he just started to run, unaware that the guard was a really good runner and caught him just as he was at the main station door. The scuffle which ensued only lasted a couple of minutes but the guard ended up with a broken nose and with blood everywhere didn't see which direction *Simon* headed once out of the station.

This occurrence wouldn't have got much attention had Jerry, the guard, not had to go to the BRI at the insistence of his superior. There he was questioned by the doctor in the A&E about how he received his injuries and the doctor had advised him to contact the police. The guard thought for a moment whether it was worth it but a pretty nurse who was there cleaning him up said she thought it was a very good idea so he agreed and let her give the police a call. Once the police arrived and one of them was an attractive female Jerry was only too cooperative in giving a statement. When asked for any distinguishing features Jerry thought for a moment and then mentioned that the guy had the most evil eyes he had ever come across.

He said "I mean they were horrible, really horrible, almost like looking at the devil!" This had made the young police woman smile which made Jerry forget his broken nose for a few minutes. They took the statement but advised Jerry that there was very little chance of apprehending the guy as they had no idea where he went or if he got on another train further down the station but they would keep a record of him and the description Jerry had given them, including the eyes. Once outside the constables smiled at one another.

"Not a hope in hell of finding that guy is there?" Denise, the young one said.

"Nah, it was probably a drunk idiot who is at home sleeping it off by now" Paul the other officer said "but we still have to file the report Denise. And don't forget the "evil eyes""! and they both sniggered a little as they got into the police car.

Simon was loose in Bristol, with very little money, a small number of cuts and bruises, nowhere to go but there were loads of revellers still around the streets just waiting for him to get involved.

CHAPTER 14

The day after Rebecca was assaulted the doctors at the hospital in Cardiff said she was fit enough to leave the hospital. She still had some bruising around the tops of her legs but as he had never penetrated her there was not problems in that area. Her dad had gone home to get her some clean clothes and she was sitting in bed reading a magazine that one of the nurses had found for her and waiting for him to come back. Sergeant Wilson popped his head round the door.

"Is it OK if I come in?" he asked. "Only I have just a few more questions if you are feeling up to it?"

"No problem" Rebecca replied. "I am feeling so much better thank you, come in and ask away, anything I can do to help you catch him before he does it again and the next victim isn't so lucky!"

At this statement, and just by looking at Rebecca he could tell she hadn't been lying to the police so any doubts the sergeant had as to her attacker's intentions to kill her flew out of the window. The thought of him ignoring her statement when she had said that she was really convinced he was going to kill her made him more determined to find the guy, and stop it happening to some other innocent girl.

"Would you mind if I send a police artist in to see you before you leave so we can get an identikit picture circulated as soon as possible?"

"Oh yes that will be fine, I feel really important now, Oh sorry, I didn't mean to sound flippant under the circumstances, I know I am glad to be alive and still intact if you know what I mean".

John Wilson smiled inwardly to himself, so relieved this poor girl survived and all thanks to Charley and Petra. She sounded so young and naive and had her whole life in front of her. I bet she won't fight with her dad for a while now, he thought , then giving her a friendly wave left the room.

Once back at the station John got straight on with getting the artist dispatched to the hospital before Rebecca left. He then called Constable Shaw, who was the other policeman who had attended Rebecca with him after the attack.

"Patrick, I have a little job for you please" he then went on to explain that he wanted Patrick to get on the computer and search for any persons on police files wanted in connection with assaults, rapes or even murders.

Firstly, though, he should print off a map of the trains that travel to Cardiff and search for the towns before Swindon that they pass through, and concentrate on those areas before any others. If there are any identikit pictures available he should print them off as a matter of priority and any descriptions too. He didn't hold out massive hope but he thought it was worth a shot.

He left him to do that while he went to write his report and then, hopefully, head to the cafeteria for a quick breakfast before it got too busy.

Well the report got done but he never managed to get to the cafeteria due to Patrick catching him up just as he was heading in that direction.

"Sarge I think I might have something"

Patrick and John sat in front of the computer screen. There, in front of them, was a police artist's impression of a very dangerous and wanted man from the Guildford area in Surrey. Wanted for a murder dating three years ago and suspected of other assaults and possibly a murder only months ago.

John immediately called the artist he had sent to Rebecca's hospital room and when he answered asked if he had completed the sketch of the assailant yet. Almost, was the reply, so John asked him to send him a copy onto the office computer just as soon as it was finished. There was just time for Patrick to dash down to the cafeteria and collect two bacon sandwiches and two coffees before the computer pinged to tell them a message had arrived. They had printed off the picture that Patrick had found on the police computer file and they then pressed the button for a print of the one attached to the message they had just received. Bingo!

The two men looked at each other and they could see the excitement in each other's eyes. John immediately picked up the phone and dialled the station in Guildford. After explaining he needed to speak to somebody about a wanted man the switchboard put him through, unknowingly and luckily to the perfect person, Toby.

"Detective Mitchell"

"Oh hi, this is Sergeant Wilson from Cardiff police, I think I am just about to make your day "!!!

Within ten minutes Oliver and Toby were throwing on their coats and heading for the door. Toby had called Orla and persuaded her, and her mother Nicky of course, to go with them down to Cardiff where they were hoping Rebecca and Orla could confirm that they were both attacked by the same man. On the journey Oliver called the hospital and asked if they would ask Rebecca to hang on until they got there.

Rebecca and her father were waiting in one of the family rooms when Toby arrived.

"Thank you for waiting for us" Toby began. "I am detective Mitchell, this is detective Marshall, this young lady" and he motioned for Orla to come forward "is Orla and this is her mother Nicky. Orla was attacked by a man we think is the same man who attacked you."

Just as Toby was talking a tall man entered the room carrying a huge bouquet of flowers and a box of Thornton's chocolates. All the eyes in the room rounded on him.

"May I ask who you are please sir"?" Toby said

"Oh yes, yes of course", the man stuttered but before he could continue Rebecca stood up and stepped forward saying

"I know who this is! Your name is Charley, isn't it, and you saved my life!" and at this she walked up to the man and threw her arms around his middle and hugged him.

Everyone started to speak at once, Toby trying to take control, Rebecca's dad trying to shake the man's hand and thank him and Charley trying to explain that is was just luck and he wasn't the hero they kept saying he was.

Once it all died down Toby got them all to sit down, well the ones that had a chair to sit on that is.

"OK," he started. "Maybe we could get the pictures we have printed off and let you ladies look and see if you agree it is the same man, also Charley, you will know too I'm sure, you said you got a good look at him didn't you? Please take your time and look very carefully as this is really important"

The three of them studied the two pictures Oliver produced and after a minute or two they all looked up at the same time. Yes definitely, they all agreed.

"Thank you" Toby said "Now I will need some details from both you ladies about him, Charley, thank you for your help but I need to speak to the girls on their own now"

"Of course of course" Charley got up to go. "I just wanted to wish Rebecca all the best" he handed her the flowers and chocolates. "Look after yourself sweetheart". He went to the door and before going out he turned and said "It was his eyes you know, they looked positively evil, that is why I came back, I'll never forget those eyes!" Rebecca's dad got up saying he would walk out with Charley as he wanted a word with him anyway.

Once they had gone the girls started talking about *Simon*. Yes he had told them both his name was *Simon*, yes he had been charming and was really good looking, had an incredible smile but they both agreed that those eyes at first meeting were kind, sparkly and warm but they could change in a second into evil. Unbelievable evil.

Toby and Oliver took all this information in and noted down anything that was useful.

"You said that you met *Simon* when he was sitting on a bench at the station Rebecca, is that correct?"

"Yes" Rebecca replied "He was sitting with a coffee and a croissant and I had looked at it thinking how much I could do with one too." She gave a sort of embarrassed smile. "He saw me looking and could tell that had been crying as I was still dabbing my eyes. He was so charming and offered me the croissant, which made me smile, and then we got chatting. I told him I was heading to Swindon but when we were on the train he persuaded me to go with him to Cardiff, honestly he could charm the birds out of the trees and at no time did I feel threatened, well not then anyway" She glanced at Orla as she said it and Orla nodded in agreement.

Once back at the police station Oliver and Toby sat together going though all the information they had gathered. There was no doubt in either of their minds that *Simon* was their man.

Toby had been to the superintendent and requested assistance on finding *Simon* and after he went through all the facts the super had agreed this *"Simon"* could well be the man that Toby had been after for the murder of his colleague years before and gave him a free rein to get full co-operation from all his staff.

Toby assembled all available officers in the main briefing room and once they were all settled with their coffees and in their seats he proceeded to tell them the whole story of *Simon*, or whoever he was for whatever occasion. Some of them had already heard about Toby's colleague who was murdered and knew about Tilly and now Toby was explaining about the latest murder and attacks it started to all make a lot of sense. They universally agreed that *Simon* must be their man.

"Now we need a plan to track him of course" Toby was saying, "firstly I want all assaults on women that have been reported but unsolved in or around any of the areas where we know he has been, say within a fifty mile radius. Maybe there is a pattern of areas he knows, it's a long shot but worth a try I think. Then I want two of you, er Pete and Colin?" he looked at the two officers sitting side by side and they both nodded "to go back through all the assaults we know about and re interview the victims just in case there is anything more we can get to work on. Also so check on any unsolved murders of young women in the last few years to see if there are any possible evidence connecting them to our man. And lastly please remember he's a slippery bastard but we are going to get him, understand, he must be caught before he can do any more damage." Then he added "and everyone, this is not only for everyone else, this is personal, my wife is in a hospital in New Zealand in a vegetable state because of this man." There was a small amount of mumbling as they all stood up as not all of them knew exactly what had happened to Tilly.

Toby and Oliver went back to their office ready to discuss their next step.

They went through all the files they had on *Simon* and listed all the victims where they actually knew it was him after the murder of (his old partner) and the distress of Tilly even though he hadn't actually attacked her he had caused her total breakdown.

So we have :-

Sam - attacked,

Sam's dad Roger, - murdered.

Orla - attacked

Rebecca – rescued

"That is four since....well you know" continued Toby. "I know there must be more out there, we just need to trace them and come up with the link that will help us find him and put him away forever. Come on Oliver, let's go through it all again and double check any area we think he might have been to more than once. There must be some sort of pattern to his movements surely or it is all just totally random. If so then we don't stand a hope in hell of catching him. Let's hope one of the guys comes up trumps with something." Just as he finished this sentence, as if by magic, the door to the office opened after a short tap and in walked Tristan, one of the younger PCs in the team.

"Thought you might be pleased to see this, Toby", Tristan said as he dropped a paper file down in front of him and then took one of the chairs on the other side of the desk. Oliver came around to Toby's side of the desk and the pair of them looked as Toby opened the file.

Inside there was a witness statement from a woman from Chertsey who had been attacked and then gagged and tied to a chair.

"It was a while ago," said Tristan, "but I thought it might be worth a second look. Her attacker was never caught. The statement explains how she had met a man in a pub. He was charming, good looking and seemed really genuine so she had gone on a date with him a couple of days later which wasn't so good so she decided not to see him again. He phoned her and eventually persuaded her to let him come round to her house for an evening so she had given him her address. When he hadn't shown up on the night he was supposed to, she had gone out with friends instead but on her return he was waiting for her outside her flat. She had supposed one of the tenants in another flat had let him in the front door. Anyway as soon as she opened the door he followed her in and hit her from behind. The next thing she knew she was bound and gagged. The statement goes on to tell the story of her flatmate breaking in and rescuing her the next day. The police had never even questioned anybody for the assault as there was such little to go on, but they had got Helen (the victim) to describe her assailant to the police sketch artist."

"Voila!" Tristan said as he held up a picture. "I think you might know who this is?"

Toby and Oliver stared at the picture of *Simon.* Tristan could not stop himself from pumping up his chest, he was rather proud of his finding. As were Toby and Oliver, "Well done Tris, I'll get you your next coffee and maybe even a biscuit!" Oliver said which made Tristan even prouder.

Toby got a map out and spread it out onto the desk in front of them. He got an orange highlighter pen and began at Guildford by circling a thirty-mile diameter area, then Exeter in Devon and Cardiff and did the same with the pen to those areas, then to Southampton where Orla was assaulted. "No pattern yet" Toby said. "Not that I was expecting one, but after him going to Devon it looks like he came back up, but then to Cardiff. So where the hell is he now? We'll have to wait and see what the others come up with."

There was nothing they could for now so they both decided they would call it a day for today.

"Are you coming back with me?" Oliver asked "I think Katie is out tonight with her yoga pals to celebrate one of their birthdays, we can have a curry and a footie match, what do you reckon?"

He asked because although Toby was staying with Oliver and his wife Katie he usually worked late and sometimes ate in the local pub. It was just to give his friends a break from him, he didn't want to encroach on their lives too much. He was looking for a place of his own but he would have to admit he hadn't been looking as hard as maybe he should. Deep down he wanted to catch this bastard as soon as possible so he could get back to his beloved Tilly. He called the hospital as often as he dared without them getting too annoyed by telling him there was no change and that they would of course let him know if there was any change no matter how slight. He also called his parents every other day just to check that they had been to see Tilly. Of course they always had as they were in the routine of going alternate days and sitting with her for about half an hour. They would read their newspapers, sometimes out aloud so Tilly could hear although they both knew that she couldn't and almost certainly never would again. Since they had moved her to a new convalescence home, with a specialist unit, nothing had changed. She just lay there in her own world. She was fed by a tube and washed and cared for by the nurses who were very kind and well trained but it was a sad sight to see. Of course when Toby phoned them they didn't say too much, just that they would sit with her and talk about what was in the newspapers, but that there was no change. Toby had got used to this stock reply and knew that if there was any change whatsoever he would be told immediately but he got comfort just talking about Tilly, even if it was not about any good news.

"I'll be there a bit later, how about I bring a ruby in with me?"

"Sounds good" Oliver replied. "Make sure you bring a naan too, love my naan, anyway where are you off to first then?"

"I just thought I would go and sit quietly with a pint and have a bit of a think, OK mate? Er, you can come if you want."

"Nah I'm fine, I'll see you at home later with the curry, don't be too long though, I'm pretty hungry" and with that he gave a little laugh and left Toby to it. He knew Toby needed a bit of "him" time now and again. He felt for his friend as he had no idea what it must be like having a wife living like a vegetable in a different country. It made him more determined though to catch this *Simon* to relieve Toby of some of his burden.

Five minutes after Oliver had left Toby started to pack up the files on his desk and was thinking where he would go for a pint when his phone rang. For a second or two Toby thought about leaving it, but then of course decided he shouldn't, so grabbed at the hand set. It was one of the policemen from downstairs in the records room, who, although he wasn't anything to do with Toby's investigation, did know all about *Simon* and what he was wanted for. He also had a girlfriend, who was a junior police officer and was currently doing work training down in Bristol.

"Er Hmm Detective Mitchell?" then continued when Toby responded with a yes.

"I have no idea if this is anything that might be useful to you, err I mean I don't want to disturb you or anything but.... well you see my girlfriend Denise is a PC and took a statement from a railway guard who had been assaulted by a man at the station where he worked, he had his nose broken. Anyway when he gave a description of the man he told my girlfriend that his assailant had evil eyes. He apparently went on about those eyes, also the assailant was very vicious. Now I know that you are looking for this *Simon* and apparently everyone says how evil his eyes are supposed to be, well I just sort of thought that maybe it was the same man. Now I've said it, it seems stupid, I am sorry if I am wasting your time but if I didn't tell you and it turned out that it was him ..." he trailed off.

"Firstly, sorry did you tell me your name?"

"Dean, sorry sir. It's Dean."

"Well Dean you are never wasting my time giving me any information so well done there" Toby said. "Now where was this station?" Once Toby realised that Bristol was on the line from Cardiff he began to get very interested. "Can you get this girlfriend of yours to give me a call as soon as possible please?"

Dean assured him that he would call his girlfriend straight away and Toby sat back down in his chair and waited for the call.

Within five minutes Toby was in conversation with Denise who was a bit worried at first in case, like Dean had said, she was wasting a senior officer's time but when Toby assured her she was doing exactly the right thing she told him all the details. When it got to the description of the man, although no picture had been sketched, the description matched *Simon* perfectly. Toby thanked her and praised her for realising the importance of her information. She was very chuffed but felt really guilty as she had just told Dean about the man and the evil eyes just for a bit of a laugh really, it was Dean that had put two and two together. Still never mind she thought, it doesn't matter how he found out, if it was useful. Toby took the details from her and asked her to organise the guard to go into the police station in Bristol the next day so he could interview him and show him the identikit sketch.

Feeling quite encouraged Toby continued to pack away his paperwork and headed for the Merry Widow, a pub nearby and quite close to the curry house, so he popped in there first and put in an order for two lamb madras, two pilau rice and two keema naans, to be ready for pick up in about an hour. He then headed to the Merry Widow. It was quiet as it was still early evening, so Toby's pint of Guinness was being pulled for him as soon as he walked in the door. "Hi Toby, usual is it?" Harry the landlord was smiling from behind the bar and placing the glass under the beer tap "Caught any good gangsters lately?"

Toby smiled back and shook his head, "Nah not today Harry, saving them up for tomorrow so you can serve a few tonight before I take them away" They both laughed and Toby picked up his beer and leaving a five pound note on the bar moved over to a chair by the log burner, meanwhile Harry went off to serve another customer who had just walked in. Toby liked a bit of solitude and liked a Guinness or two so this pub suited him perfectly. It never got crowded before at least nine, and Harry was quite happy not to bother the customers with his inane chat unless they wanted him to.

He sat for two pints thinking firstly about Tilly and then on to the new information he had just received from Bristol. His mind was full so he decided it was time to head to the curry house, pick up the food and relax at Oliver's for a while.

Oliver had plates warmed and beers poured when Toby arrived, a football match he had recorded earlier was set up on the TV, set for a boys night. Toby smiled to himself as he saw it all setup, Oliver was a great bloke, and he was glad to have him as a mate.

They scoffed the curries and beers in no time and were just putting to rights the terrible passes some of the football players had made when Toby's mobile went off.

Oliver watched his best mate crumble before his eyes as he listened to the voice on his phone.

After what seemed like a lifetime Toby put down his phone, and with tears streaming from eyes looked up at Oliver and told him that Tilly had given up her will to live and had stopped breathing two hours ago. That the doctors had tried to save her but had failed. He was now a widower.

Oliver jumped up hugged his friend. There was nothing he could do or say that would help, just a comforting arm around the shoulder was all he could do. They stayed like that for quite a few minutes, saying nothing, Toby letting out a sob now and again. Oliver with tears in his eyes too, trying to imagine the remotest idea of what Toby must be feeling.

After a while Toby pulled away and dried his eyes, "Well that's it then" he said in a shaky voice. "At least she is free now."

CHAPTER 15

Simon needed to get some money and fast, his fifty pound note was not going to last long. He went to a Travel Lodge he had spotted when he arrived near the station and went to book a room for one night, but it was going to cost him all of his fifty pounds, so he left telling the receptionist he would be back later, after he had been to collect his wages. He marvelled at just how good he was at thinking up lies so fast. Such gullible people, or maybe just not interested anyway. Once outside he looked around to find the nearest pub. Always a good place to either pick up a lonely soul and use them or to steal a wallet or two. Pick pocketing had become quite an art with him since his school days although he rarely needed to use it now, what with all the foolish women, or even men, around who he could take advantage of in all ways !

He ventured into the Smugglers Arms which was so crowded he hardly managed to get to the bar but by the time he did he had already got two wallets neatly stashed in his pocket. He ordered a pint of Guinness as it takes a long time to pull and told the bar maid he would be back in a few minutes. This gave him time to go to the gents and lock himself into a cubical to check out his spoils. Just as he was doing that a couple of blokes came in. One of them was telling the other that he had lost his wallet. *Simon* froze for a second.

"Aw you bloody idiot" the other guy said "You must have left it on the table in the curry house. They both relieved themselves and then left allowing *Simon* to breathe again.

He drank his pint quickly, just in case anything kicked off although he thought he was pretty safe, and headed back to the Travel Lodge. The same girl was on reception and *Simon* booked a room for two nights with the option to increase his stay if necessary. He didn't think the girl even recognised him from earlier as she was far too busy checking her phone for whatever. Lazy rude bitch, *Simon* thought, I may have to pay her a visit while I'm in the area.

His room was fair, comfortable enough. It had a bathroom, bed and TV so what more could he want? The two wallets he had stolen produced a lot more that he expected. He now had over two hundred pounds, excluding the fifty in his shoe. Great result he thought, why would people go out with a load of cash on them with people like me around? That thought made him laugh to himself. He had no intentions of using any of the cards though as he didn't want to take any chances, he had got away with it before but didn't want to risk it again.

He lay on the bed and fell asleep almost instantly.

Simon awoke to the sun shining through the thin beige curtains. He could hear the noise of the morning staff banging plates and trays around as his room was unfortunately only about twenty yards from the kitchen. Still, no time for lying in he thought, lots to do today. Sort out some more money, somewhere to stay and some lucky person to sponge off. He was getting a bit restless too, having had to give up on his attempted conquest of the stupid bird in Cardiff. His need for some excitement was coming to the fore again.

It was only 7.30am but he was hungry and wide awake so he showered and locking the door of his room after him, headed to the cafeteria a few feet away. The staff had made coffee in a filter machine and had laid out croissants and bread rolls next to jams and butters. There was a small selection of cereals and a jug of milk but not a lot else. The sign on the wall said £6 for what was on offer but a cooked breakfast was available at a cost of £10 if you asked the staff.

Simon was starving so he selected a full English from the menu offered to him by the girl he had originally met when he booked in. At least she spoke a little to him this time and her phone wasn't in sight. When she brought his breakfast she smiled. Well, he thought to himself, she's actually not half bad.

He finished eating and poured himself another cup of coffee. The cafeteria was half full by this time. There were a couple of tables with hen and stag parties sitting at them, boasting about just how mush booze they had managed to consume the night before. Girls were giggling while re enacting the previous evening's antics.

Simon watched thinking to himself what a shower of crap. Suddenly a voice from his side broke into his thoughts.

"Can I get you anything else?" the girl from reception was asking him. "I can get you some more toast if you like, you certainly finished that breakfast fast!"

Simon looked up at the girl, yes, he though, she is OK. "That would be lovely" he said. "Maybe you could join me?"

Greta blushed "Well I am due a tea break in ten minutes, shall I bring your toast then so I can join you?"

Result, *Simon* thought to himself as he nodded and told her that sounded good. He even added one of his heart warming smiles.

Greta brought his toast and another cup of coffee for each or them. She introduced herself and within the twenty minutes of her break they had got to know each other. Greta told *Simon* that she shared a flat with a girlfriend, that she was only working at the Travel Lodge while she saved enough money up to go travelling. *Simon* made up a great story about how he had left his flat after he found out his wife had been cheating on him with his best friend, how he had tried to make a go of their relationship, and how she had secretly cleaned out his bank account. He certainly knew how to lay on a story very convincingly. He had her eating out of his hand.

They arranged to meet later that day in a pub Greta suggested. *Simon*, feeling very smug about just how fast he could create a different past life, was thinking he might have a bed for a few more nights too. Hmmm and even more !!!!

He strolled around Bristol for a while trying to work out just which shop was best to do a little more pick pocketing. He knew that now most shops were fitted with cameras so he had to pick ones that were either really crowded, or where it was obvious that no security guards were present, just in case he had to run. He had no intention of getting caught for some petty crime. If he was going to get caught, which he assumed he never would, it would be in a blaze of glory and he would be renowned for his atrocities, such as the likes of Jack the Ripper or Fred West were remembered. But this was never going to happen because he was too clever for the likes of the stupid police in England.

With these thoughts he picked up his stride and marched into Primark with a total air of confidence. It was a Friday and the store was pretty full of women with buggies and pre school children running circles around them. Easy pickings *Simon* thought as the women rarely noticed their bags were easy to open, they were far too busy looking for something to wear for themselves or their horrible brats running around. Then all of a sudden, and only for a second, Tyler appeared in *Simon*s head. It was just as he had lifted a nice fat purse from a woman's open shopping bag. She was busy comforting a crying baby and as she leaned over cooing at the child Tyler's part of his brain remembered his own baby. *Simon* soon pushed the thought away. There was no room in his brain for the weak and pathetic Tyler, who would never have stolen the purse or if he had would now be thinking of putting it back. *Simon* actually laughed out loud at this thought and the woman with the crying baby looked up at him.

Quickly he moved away, he didn't want anybody remembering his face for any reason.

By the time he left the shop he was carrying eight purses and a money clip that he had managed to take from a rather weird looking guy who was looking at women's underwear. *Simon* knew he would be perfect for the steal as he was looking so nervous himself, maybe he was stealing too.

He went to the nearest coffee bar and found a table right at the back where he could see all the comings and goings but hardly anybody could see much of him. Here he proceeded to check his spoils. Wow it must be pay day today he thought as he emptied out the purses. Seven hundred and twenty pounds he had collected. Although half of that had been from the weird man's money clip. After all who the hell carries a money clip now a days, he deserved to have it nicked. He ordered himself a large flat white from the counter and went back to sit down again. He was half way through it when the woman whose baby had been crying came into the cafe. She had two friends with her and of course the screaming brat and another toddler hanging onto her arm. The three of them settled around a table about half way down the cafe. One of the women went up to order while the others were chatting. The all of a sudden there was a shriek. Everyone looked at the women. The one with the baby was frantically searching through her bag, then the buggy, then her pockets and grabbing the small amount of shopping she had in the big brown Primark bag, emptied the contents onto the cafe table.

"It's definitely not here" she was saying to her friends, "it had a whole week's benefit money, one hundred and eighty pounds. What am I going to do?" and the tears started to spill. Her friends were trying to console her, saying that she might have dropped it somewhere and it would be handed in and not to get too upset until they had checked everywhere. One of the women went off to ask in the shops whilst the other sat with her friend as the waitress brought them both their coffees. The child had stopped crying at least even if the woman had not. The toddler, in its favour, was just wandering around the room not making a sound. That was until it walked up to *Simon*.

"Go away" *Simon* hissed at the boy "Go back to your mummy" but the child just stood looking at him, the way children do. "I said go away" *Simon* repeated, but as he did so a tiny bit of his brain said shhhhhhhh. It was Tyler he was sure so he pushed hard and the shhh went away. Then he said to the child again "Go away!" this time a little louder, just in case the child was hard of hearing. The child didn't move and *Simon* was beginning to get a bit annoyed. He decided to go, but just as he stood up, he dropped two of the purses off his lap. They were both now empty of course but they made a noise as they fell. *Simon* now had two choices, either bend to pick them up or just go, leaving them where they fell, and hope that nobody noticed them fall. He chose the latter. He got up and began, sidling around the boy who hadn't moved, and began to head for the door. He was just passing the women at their table when the one with the baby looked up at him, a brief flicker of recognition then turned away. Just at that moment the child cried out "Hay mummy here's your purse!" The woman looked around just as her brat of a child was toddling towards here carrying one of the purses *Simon* had dropped. "That man found it" he said pointing to *Simon.*

Again two choices, did he stand and blag it or carry one walking as if he had heard nothing. He again chose the latter and despite a few shouts from the cafe he just went through the door and lost himself into the crowd of shoppers outside. He walked a short distance before he ducked into another big shop and was invisible once again.

Back in the cafe the women all exchanged looks at one another. Jodie, the woman who had lost her purse took the second purse her son was offering her and put it on the table.

"Do you think it was that man who took my purse?" she asked her friend "it seems a bit strange that he had found two, he must have pinched it out of my bag!"

"And somebody else's by the looks of things" her friend Catherine said looking at the other purse on the table.

Both purses were empty of cash but still had the odd bits of paperwork, like odd receipts and supermarket loyalty cards, and the other one had a drivers licence in it.

As the women were looking a them a man came over to their table.

"Hi ladies" both women looked up at a tall middle aged man looking down on them.

"I'm sorry to interrupt you but I might be able to help. My name is Jim Forester and I am a police officer. OK, I am off duty at the moment" pointing to his jeans and sweatshirt with a logo about loving dogs on it, "but I couldn't fail to overhear your conversation, oh and of course your scream!" he paused for a moment while the ladies smiled a little.

"Can I ask you to not touch the purses any more. We have had a spate of pick pocketing in this area and I might be able to get some prints off one or both of them which might help us find out who is doing it" He motioned to the waitress, who was hovering, trying to catch exactly what was going on, to come closer and then asked her if she would find a plastic bag for him to put the items in.

"I'm afraid I'm going to have to ask you ladies to come down to the station and have your prints taken so we can exclude them from any we find. "Also your husband's madam" he said to Jodie.

"No you won't need his" Jodie said rather bitterly. "I haven't seen him in months and he sure has never been near this purse" she glanced at Catherine as if to say she would always keep her purse hidden from him anyway. Catherine knew exactly that she meant and nodded slightly.

"OK then" Jim continued, "can you pop down to Leyland Road police station as soon as you can and we can get a statement from you about the theft and finger prints at the same time. Did you see anybody, the guy that left as your son found your purse, did you recognise him?"

Jodie thought for a moment and then she realised she did, well she was almost sure she did.

“I think I saw him in Primark, yes I am sure it was him, he was staring at me with evil eyes while I was seeing to the baby. I just thought he was annoyed because the baby was making a noise but, heh he must have been sussing out my bag. He moved off as soon as I gave him an evil stare back”

The baby started to grizzle at that point and the little boy, who had been so quiet all the time the conversations were going on, started to whine. Jim carefully put the purses in the bags the waitress had provided for him and suggested they all got off, and that he would see them at the station when they could get themselves there. Tears had formed in Jodie's eyes as she thought of her lost money. Jim could see her distress and was a kind soul so he took a five pound note from his wallet and handed it to Jodie.

“Here take the bus home, I’m sure your friends will help sort you out” he said

Jodie thanked him, although Catherine said she would have paid for the bus Jim just waved her away and said it was his treat. A few minutes later the girls' other friend came back into the cafe. She said she had been to all the shops they had visited but no luck in finding the purse. Then looked at them all as they said there was a tale to be told on the way home.

Simon was really annoyed with himself for being so stupid. That was twice now he had been noticed. Was he losing his grip?. Twice now he had heard Tyler in his head, and twice he had dropped his guard for a second. He needed to keep Tyler completely out of the picture, but how...Tyler was part of his brain, he was in his head. How can you destroy part of your own head!

He made his way to the pub where he had arranged to meet Greta. He was a little early but thought it was probably best to get off the street for a while anyway. He bought a pint of Guinness and a packet of peanuts, grabbed one of the copies of the daily papers that were left out for the customers to read and sat at one of the corner tables where he got a good view of the main door. He wanted to check none of the women came in, although he knew that was very unlikely.

He sat reading the rubbish in the paper for about an hour and was on his second pint before Greta appeared. She seemed delighted to see him, almost as if she hadn't been sure whether he was going to show up or not. She motioned to the bar and pointed to his half empty glass, he nodded and sat back thinking hmmm bed for the night almost guaranteed, and lots more too maybe !

They sat chatting in the pub for another hour and after consuming maybe a few more drinks than they should have Greta announced that she was starving and how about they go and get a curry or something? She didn't have to work that night so they had the whole evening free.

And the night too! *Simon* was hoping.

They wandered down towards the river Avon and found The Little Taste of India open and only half full. Greta was true to her statement of her being starving and ordered poppadums and onion bhajis to start followed by a lamb madras curry and pilau rice and a garlic naan bread She then turned to *Simon* as if she had forgotten he was there.

"What are you having then? I had better warn you I don't share my food" and she giggled. It was probably only the wine she had been drinking that made her like this but suddenly *Simon* felt he didn't like her so much any more !!

He just ordered a lamb curry and a plain naan and then sat while Greta wolfed down her starters as soon as they arrived. There was ample for two really but she didn't so much as even offer him a mouthful. *Simon* was beginning to get just a little pissed off.

He waited until both their meals had arrived before ordering a bottle of wine. He knew Greta was a bit tipsy and thought he would top her up just in case he needed her a little more malleable later.

She had no trouble in downing most of the bottle of wine, in fact *Simon* had to almost wrestle the bottle from her hand to even top up his glass just the once. You'll pay for this later my girl, the thought was in his head.

It was dark when they left the restaurant and beginning to rain slightly but there were still loads of people about. He had decided he no longer wanted to wheel his way into staying at her place as she was annoying him far too much. No, a new plan had been forming while she was stuffing her face with curry and now he had to carry it out, but he needed to find the right place.

They walked past the crowds and towards the bridge over the Avon. Greta was swaying a bit as she walked and clung onto *Simon* to keep herself steady. The warmth of her body against his felt quite good and his erection started to present itself. This almost made him change his plan but when he thought back to her stuffing naan bred into her mouth and the spittle coming out as she tried to speak through it, his erection ebbed and his plan fell back into place.

The rain had started to get heavier as they crossed over the bridge so *Simon* pulled Greta into the first piece of shelter they got to. It was the remains of an old hut, probably used to house maintenance equipment years ago but now almost collapsed but still with a small amount of roof and a couple of walls intact. Perfect spot, went thought his mind. He pushed her against the wall which was not too easy as she was wobbling a bit and her knees wanted to buckle. This annoyed him greatly as his erection had returned once she hadn't been spitting naan at him for a while and he decided he was going in for a fuck against the wall. But with her like this it meant he would have to lie her down. Still what did he care if it was wet on the ground, after all it was her that would feel the wet and not for long anyway. This thought made him smile. He looked left and right to check there were no nosey dog walkers like the last time, or revellers on their way home from wherever they had been partying. All was clear so he pushed Greta down onto the ground. She resisted of course,

"No not here!" she said trying to push him away. "Anyway I am not up for that, I think I should go home now!"

Greta didn't go home. Greta didn't have a chance to do anything. *Simon's* fist hit her like a sledge hammer straight in her face. She was out cold in less than a second. She was raped whilst laying on the cold wet ground unconscious and then smothered by *Simon* sitting on her face until no breath was left inside her. All this time he was laughing to himself. New novel way to getting rid of rubbish he thought.

He walked away not even bothering to cover her lifeless body. Nobody was around, nobody cared. He was invincible, he was the greatest.

CHAPTER 16

By 4.30pm the day after Toby received his devastating news that Tilly had died, he was on a plane bound for New Zealand, one short stopover meant that he would be with her by Wednesday afternoon. With her, he thought, no not with her, just with her memory. After all she had left him two days earlier. Toby wasn't a religious guy and had no beliefs in any afterlife but he was yearning to see her, to say a proper goodbye. He supposed he had been waiting for this to happen for so long that he had almost dismissed the idea that it actually would. He knew when he left for the UK that he wasn't going to find her killer and go back and make her better, that was all a dream. He knew it was as soon as he uttered the words to his friend but it was a dream he could hang on to even though he knew it was never going to be fulfilled because he knew deep down, that in reality, Tilly had left him a long time ago.

Oh yes, he thought, if it was possible he was even more determined to catch the bastard who caused all this misery, and yes with any luck he would get the chance to kill him himself.

Toby stayed in New Zealand for a week, just enough time to say goodbye to his beloved Tilly and visit with his parents. Then to take some flowers to the lovely nurse Suzie Tompak to say a big thank you for all she had done in taking care of Tilly in those early days. She had attended the cremation and had hugged Toby in genuine grief at the end of the tiny service. Toby had insisted on no priest or vicar spouting off about what a wonderful person Tilly was as no such clergy had ever met her, but he did allow anybody who wanted to, to say a few words. That ended up being his father and himself and a few kind words from Suzie. Tilly was unknown to any other relations Toby had in New Zealand, although a few of the distant cousins had sent cards. His friend Daniel had attended and had hugged Toby too but as he had never met Tilly there wasn't a lot he could say.

His parents tried to get him to stay for a while but Toby had nothing left in New Zealand now, other than them. He said he hoped they understood, which of course they did, and so he left on the first flight he could get booked on. All that was on his mind was to get back to the UK and find the fiend who had wrecked so many lives. He hoped his colleagues had been working on any leads in his absence. They had told him they would not be contacting him while he was away as they said he would need time to grieve. They thought it was the right thing to do but Toby wanted to know what was going on, he needed to know, it was only the thought of finding *Simon* that kept him sane and kept him going.

After the cremation Toby had gone back to his parents house, locked himself away and in a study and had cried all his tears. He had promised Tilly, in his mind, that the man who had done this to her and to so many others would be caught and that at the end of the chase the man would be dead.

CHAPTER 17

Oliver was at Heathrow and as soon as Toby got though customs he saw his friend waiting. He was really glad to see him, not only to catch up on anything that had happened while he was away but also he wanted a mate, a real mate. It almost brought more tears to his eyes to see him waiting for him and looking so happy to see him.

They hadn't walked more that ten feet before Toby started. "Any news?" he asked.

"Blimey you don't waste any time do you?" Oliver replied. "Yes, but at least wait until we get to the car so I can think straight!" He patted Toby on the shoulder.

Once driving Oliver explained that they had sent the picture off to the station guard who was attacked in Bristol and he had identified *Simon* as his attacker so another mark on their map.

"So do you think he is still in Bristol?" Toby said "after all it was a couple of weeks ago now since that attack happened, he could be anywhere now."

"Well yes, and it's sad to say that we won't know unless or until there is another attack I suppose" Oliver said.

Toby didn't want to go back to Oliver's and suggested they go straight to the station. After all it was 8.30am and he had insisted he'd slept on the plane, even though both of then knew he hadn't.

Once in the office and with a Costa and a Danish pastry apiece they started to go through their lists again adding the Bristol attack. They had just written the word Bristol when Chief Inspector Collins walked into the office. Both officers looked up at once to see the Chief staring down at them.

"I have just had a call from a Sergeant Jennings in Bristol, apparently yesterday they discovered the body of a young woman, they suspect she was murdered. It looks like she has been dead for less than 36 hours, we will know more once the autopsy has been completed but I thought you guys should know as it may be connected to the case you are working on. I understand the last sighting on your man was Bristol?"

Oliver and Toby looked at each other and you could almost feel the excitement in their looks.

They both stood at the same time and Toby grabbed their files and Oliver his car keys and they were out of the door before they could hear the Chief Inspector wish them luck or hear him call "Glad you're back Toby!"

"So the Chief has been reading his emails then?" Toby said as they pulled out of the police station car park, I always thought he just put them in the trash!"

"Oh ha ha" Oliver said. "He was very interested when I updated him on all we knew and the addition of the Bristol attack. He's one of the good guys you know."

They headed straight for the motorway and the direction of Bristol.

“This could be the break we’ve been hoping for!” Oliver said as they turned onto the M4. “Well, not a break for the girl who has been murdered of course.”

“Well we don’t know if that is the case yet Oliver” Toby replied. “But if it turns out she was murdered we might have a better chance of catching the bastard if he is still in the Bristol area.”

They stopped, just for five minutes, at Membury services. Just so Oliver could pop to the loo and Toby could grab them both a coffee. While he was waiting in the queue to be served his phone rang. It was Sergeant Jennings.

The preliminary results on the cause of death of the poor girl found on the bridge had come through.

Toby had tears in his eyes when Oliver appeared two minutes later.

“Is the coffee that bad?” he began but then could see the state Toby was in “What's the matter mate?” he said, concerned and putting a hand on Toby's shoulder.

“She was murdered” Toby said. “I have just had a call, they think she was raped and then by the sound of things he must have just sat on her face until she stopped breathing. There was obviously a struggle. My god does this bastard have no limits?”

“Well” began Oliver “At least he might have left some DNA or evidence of some sort this time, lets hang on to that thought.”

Toby gave his friend a reassuring nod as they headed back to their car.

Sergeant Jennings was waiting in his office for them when they arrived.

"Bloody terrible business this" he said as they walked in. "Poor girl was in a horrible mess when she was found. Nobody deserves to end their days like that."

Both men nodded as a short almost respectful silence fell on the office.

"Right," Toby started "What do we have so far?"

Jennings looked down at his notes, "Well we know here name was Greta Marshall. She was a bit of a loner by all accounts according to her colleagues, she worked at the Travel Lodge in Park street. Had a small bed sit in Gloucester road, we have some men down there now checking it out. No parents that we have any idea about. Her friend Allison who she worked with said a guy had stayed at the Lodge last Thursday night and that she had taken her tea break with him on Friday morning after serving him breakfast. She said he seemed OK although she had noticed his eyes were very angry looking. Not that noticing somebody's eyes looking strange should imply that there is something wrong, should it?"

At this statement Toby and Oliver exchanged glances.

"We need to find this guy" Oliver said "even if it is just to eliminate him" but inside he was thinking the same as Toby.....this is our man.

The three of them sat for the next hour going through the statements of Greta's colleagues. Sergeant Jennings, or Bill as he had told them to call him, had given them all the details of how she was found by two school boys. Apparently they were bunking off school and had noticed the half derelict shed in a little dip in the ground just at the end of the suspension bridge. They had just lit a joint and as it had begun to rain thought they would pop inside while they smoked it. It had taken a while to get them to explain why they were there in the first place but when Bill had explained that he wouldn't be pressing any charges re the joint they were more talkative.

They said that Paul (the braver of the two boys) had gone in first to check that there were no tramps or anybody lurking inside. He had turned to call

Tom to follow when he tripped over what he at first had assumed was a pile of rags somebody had dumped but when Tom got inside and the both looked with their phone lights they realised it was a woman. They immediately called the police and thought of running before they could arrive because of the joint which Paul put on the ground and trod on, but Tom had said no. They might as well stay as they had used his phone to call the cops and it would be totally traceable. If they ran away they might be blamed for what ever happened to the poor woman lying on the ground. But as an afterthought added, "And we might even be famous". Totally forgetting about the joint or the playing hooky from school.

Bill had said he was sure the boys knew nothing more, they were both pretty scared of being told off for being there in the first place but I think it was lucky it rained and they were trying to smoke a joint or it might have been goodness knows how long before she was found.

"Have you managed to trace any family yet ?" Oliver had just posed the question when the door opened and a young PC entered the office.

"Sorry to disturb you sir" he said looking at Bill "but I have just found another address for that dead girl!"

Brilliant" Bill said " but can you please refer to her as something other than that dead girl, deceased sounds far more human."

The young PC went scarlet and both Toby and Oliver felt for the poor lad. Still we all have to learn Toby thought.

"Sorry sir, the girls name was Greta Marshall as we already know from her work, but her original name was Greta Phillips. She changed it by deed poll about six months ago. That is why we couldn't trace her at first, but I spoke again with her friend Allison and she mentioned that her step father's name was Phillips but she despised him for some reason so changed her name when she left home. She also said she thought that Greta had actually left home without telling anybody. Well I ran a few checks and found a girl called Greta Phillips was reported missing from her home in Weston Super Mare around seven months ago. It hadn't been followed up much as she was almost nineteen although the mother appeared to be very concerned about her as she had contacted the police station on several occasions. It was never followed up as there was no reason to think there was anything wrong, just a teenager getting away from her parents."

"Right then" Toby said. "We will have to go and see her parents, we don't want the news people getting onto it before we tell them. This is the part of the job I hate"

"Do you want me to organise that?" Bill said. "I can get a police woman to go and see them."

"No its fine" Toby continued, "although we will take a female officer with us and maybe you could contact their local family liaison person to go around and see that they are alright after we have been."

Bill called Sarah, a PC from the outer office and explained that she would be going with Toby. Then he arranged for Oliver to have access to the statements they had collated.

Toby and Sarah got into his car and he set the sat nav for the Phillips address.

"How long have you been in the force?" he asked her once they were on the road.

"Two years" Sarah replied "Don't worry I have done this horrible job, not the police force" she quickly added, "I mean having to tell people bad news before."

"I was just making conversation" Toby said. "I wasn't checking to see if you were up for the job!"

"Oh" Sarah said. "I didn't think you were, well maybe I did, sorry!"

"Well now we got that straightened out lets just get on eh?"

They arrived mid afternoon, the rain had started to come down in buckets and they ran from the car to the house but were still soaked by the time the front door was opened.

It was a normal type of house, semi detached, neat from the outside messy from inside. There were children's toys scattered everywhere, and a strong smell of alcohol and stale tobacco.

When Mrs Phillips answered the door she looked very confused when Toby showed her his ID, introduced Sarah and asked if they could come in. Then once inside it must have suddenly dawned on her what was happening and she immediately pre empted what he was there for.

Moving some soft toys from the settee she motioned them to sit down just as a toddler entered the room dragging a puppy by its collar.

"Let Moby go!" Mrs Phillips shouted at the child. "You'll strangle the poor thing!"

The child let go of the pup and it scampered off back into another room.

Mrs Phillips picked up the boy and sat him on her knee.

"OK tell me the worst, what has our Greta been saying now? If she's trying to say my husband did things to her she's lying, he would never do...." but the look on Sarah face stopped her mid sentence.

"Mrs Phillips" Toby began. "I am so very sorry to tell you that we have found the body of a girl who we believe to be Greta."

Sarah stood up then and gently took the child from his mother's lap saying they could go and look for the puppy.

Toby watched as Mrs Phillips digested what he had just told him and then the tears started to appear.

"Is Mr Phillips due home anytime soon?" Toby said "If not could we perhaps get a neighbour to come around?"

"He's upstairs" she said "Asleep"

"Well should I go and wake him?"

"No!" she almost shouted "I mean not yet, let him finish his sleep, Peter needs his sleep".

Toby was shocked at this. Here was a woman, who had just heard that her daughter was dead, not wanting to wake up her husband, and she hadn't even asked how her daughter had died.

Eventually Mrs Phillips looked up from her lap, tears streaming down her face.

"What happened?" she said. "I mean was it a drug overdose or an accident or something?"

Toby leaned forward and took one of her hands, "I am afraid she was murdered" he said.

At this, the change in her was almost violent. She jumped up and started pacing the room.

"How, why, what the fuck happened?" more a statement than a question.

All this noise must have woken up her husband Peter because suddenly the door flew open and a very angry looking man burst into the room.

"What the fuck is all this shouting about, I told you I wanted to sleep!" this was addressed to his wife. He appeared not to have noticed the two other people sitting in the room. He looked firstly at Sarah who had returned and was still holding onto the child, and then to Toby. Sarah's uniform must have suddenly made the penny drop as to who the visitors were and he started again"

“OK what's going on, has the cow been saying things about me ? I never did nothing to her, you mustn't believe anything she says , she's a compulsive liar you know.....”

Before he could say anything more Mrs Phillips stared at him with a face like thunder. "She's bloody dead you moron, shut up about her, she's been murdered!” and with that she sat down hard onto the chair and putting her face into her hands she started to scream almost silently into them.

About now Toby would have expected anybody normal to rush to his wife to comfort her and then to ask Toby all sorts of questions but not Peter. He just turned and headed out of the room and before Toby could say a word they heard the front door slam.

“I am really sorry Mrs Phillips“ Toby started. “But I am going to have to ask you some questions and also we will need somebody to come and identify the person we believe is your daughter.”

At this Mrs Phillips looked up “ You believe to be?” She said. “I mean Is there any doubt?“

“Sorry” Toby said. “There is no doubt” he was thinking to himself he couldn't really have just said to identify the body could he, but for a second he might have given her false hope that maybe it wasn't Greta and for that he was sorry.

Sarah was still holding onto the little lad who had been totally silent during all the shouting but was now wriggling to get down to go to his mother. Sarah put the boy down and said she would go and make some tea. Mrs Phillips took hold of her son and stroking his head soothed him. It was only when she looked hard at Toby he noticed the black bruising around her eyes and on her neck.

“Is there a relative or close neighbour we could get to come around and maybe look after the little one while I ask you some questions?” Toby asked as gently as he could.

The woman nodded, "Michelle next door should be home, I have her number here" and she picked up a book from the little table beside her chair and handed it to Toby, "It's under M for Michelle."

Michelle arrived within minutes and sat with her friend while Toby explained what had happened.

"Where's Peter?" Michelle asked "He should be here too.

Greta's mum just looked at her "Guess where he is" she said "he'll be down at the Four Feathers of course, hiding."

Toby asked if Michelle would mind taking the little boy out for a walk so he could have a chat with Mrs Phillips.

Once they were alone Toby got out his note pad, and accepting the cup of tea Sarah had just brought in for them all , started to ask his questions.

Mrs Phillips or Mary as was her name, told him she hadn't heard from Greta for months. She explained that they had reported her missing but the police hadn't been too concerned as she was over eighteen, and of course due to the reason Mary had given them which had caused the big family row.

This turned out to be an allegation from Greta of Peter, her step father, trying to rape her. He had totally denied it and had accused Greta of making up a terrible story to make her mum hate him. When the police asked Mary just how much truth there might be in the story she had sided with her husband and said that Greta constantly lied about things and that there was absolutely no truth in the tale. They must have been convinced as they took no action, just put it down to a family feud that would sort itself out.

Toby looked at Mary and very gently asked if she in fact believed that it was rubbish ? At this Mary broke down again and started to sob.

"I did think it was rubbish at first" she said once she had composed herself "but now I am not so sure. Not that it matters now though does it, my little girl is dead" and she started to sob again.

Sarah put a comforting arm around her and quietly said "If you need help Mary, we can take you to a safe house"

"No!" Mary almost shouted."If you mean Peter hurting me, he doesn't mean it, he is always really sorry afterwards" then after a few moments thought she continued "Where could we go, I mean he would find me wherever I went and then it would be twice as bad!"

"No Mary" Sarah said "we can find you a safe house and we can get him arrested for hurting you. Does he ever hit the boy? "

"No, well I have never seen him, he shouts a lot, especially when he has had a few drinks. It was his fault Greta left and now she's dead. If I had believed her we would never have had that row and she would still be here and alive . My god it was all his fault...or was it mine!!!!!"

They left leaving Michelle promising to take Mary and the boy next door to her house and that if there was any bother she would phone Sarah straight away. She said she would come with Mary the following day to identify Greta. Toby said they would send a car to collect them at 11.00am.

Once in the car on the way back to Bristol Toby asked Sarah what she made of Peter.

"I reckon the rape accusation was probably true" she said. "He looks like a wrong 'un to me. He wasn't going to hang around once he saw us, was he? You don't think he might have had anything to do with Greta's murder do you?"

"If I wasn't pretty sure that the guy we have been chasing after for the past three years is the one who did this I would definitely suspected him, but no, the guy that did this, I am sure is called *Simon* and is a very dangerous man. He has killed several people that we know about and god knows how many that we don't. We have a description and know he was in Bristol recently. Once the girl at the travel lodge who saw Greta and some guy having breakfast together sees the picture I am sure she will recognise him. Well I really hope she does and then we will know exactly if it was him or not. If by any chance it isn't him then you can be sure I am going to go and see Peter again, but this time he will not be running off to the pub!"

When they got back to the station and reported everything to Oliver he produced copies of all the pictures they had from all the different peoples descriptions of *Simon*.

The first girl who was attacked , tied up but found by her flat mate

Sam, who had a very vague looking wedding picture of her husband

The girl who was attacked and saved by the dog walker

The guard at the station in Cardiff

All the pictures looked like the same man.

Toby and Oliver went together to see Greta's friend at the Travel Lodge and after at least ten seconds she confirmed it was the guy she had seen that morning with Greta.

"OK" Oliver said " He is probably still here in Bristol, what next is just how are we going to find him!"

CHAPTER 18

As soon as *Simon* had fled from killing Greta he had rushed back to his room at the Travel Lodge, had a shower and bagged up the clothes he had been wearing into two bin liners. He slept the night, a peaceful sleep, no remorse. Not once did he think of the corpse lying in the little shed by the bridge. Not once did he think of the sounds Greta had made as he suffocated her. When he awoke the next morning fully refreshed he left the lodge. Tossing the bags of his bagged up clothes into the nearest restaurant rubbish bin.

As he walked along he gave himself a pat on the back for not only the murder but the dumping of his clothes. He was getting quite expert at all this he thought to himself. One day when I get a moment I will sit down and actually count up just how many people I have killed. And of course got away with killing. Smiling to himself he decided that if he wanted to remain uncaught he would have to move on now. Although he didn't think anybody knew who he actually was and was after him he mustn't be complacent because that is when things could go bad. He remembered that he had been seen with Greta having breakfast so better to be safe than sorry and move on.

Staring up at the railway departure board *Simon* noticed a tall blond girl doing the exact same only a yard or two away. He noticed there was a train leaving platform seven going to Reading at 10.30am. Turning to the blond and giving his special smile he asked if she too was heading for Reading,. She smiled back and was just about to answer when a guy came up behind her and handed her a coffee.

"It is on time? " he asked

She turned and replied saying "Oh you made it , I was just about to go without you"

Simon walked off quickly. Hmm he thought to himself, that would have been too good to be true.

Little would that girl ever know how near she might have been to being murdered.

Simon caught that next train to Reading. He knew it was a big town and not that far from Guildford which is a town he knew well and would probably head back to some day when everything had been forgotten about Sam and her dad. The very tiny piece of Tyler emerged when *Simon* put Guildford into his brain and Tyler thought of the babies he had left behind. Well Dylan, anyway. He wasn't sure what had happened to the other baby as it hadn't been born before *Simon* had taken over. "Fuck off" *Simon* told Tyler, who immediately went back into his box at the very base of *Simon*s brain.

Reading looked fun. *Simon* got off the train in a very light hearted mood. There were loads of people about, all the shops were busy. Lots of pockets for the picking and lots of purses for the taking he thought to himself. I need some new clothes, he thought, but before that I am starving, breakfast is the order of the day so he headed for Wetherspoon's in the centre of town. He knew he could get a great all day breakfast there for loads less than a tenner.

He ordered the full works and coffee and took a table by the window so he would watch his new victims walk by. Primark was only a few metres away and his victims were piling in there like it was an oasis in the desert. Mums with buggies were the best as they spent less time watching their bags and more time shutting up their brats while they rummaged through the hangers searching for bargains. Contrary to belief he got most of his pickings from mums. They always seemed to have a purses full of money.

He had just finished off his breakfast and felt great. Then was just deciding whether to get another coffee or head off to find somewhere to stay for the night when two girls asked if he minded if they shared his table.

He decided on another coffee.

Within twenty minutes he had found out both their names, where they were heading, what they liked to do in the evening and why they weren't at college that day. They weren't at college because they were in fact school girls, well both were just sixteen, or so they said as they giggled their way through sausage sandwiches and half shandies.

Now *Simon* had never been one to get presents and now he had two. Wrapped up and ready to be opened at his leisure. What a lucky man he was.

They chatted for about another hour and then they said they would have to be off but agreed to meet him that evening outside Skippers, the music bar in the centre of town, at 8.30pm. *Simon* couldn't believe his luck really. After all he was now a man in his 30's but could still pull school girls.

He wandered around Reading for a while until he spotted a good old Travel Lodge just on the edge of the main street, it was next door to a Holiday Inn and *Simon* was tempted to go there but then he thought he didn't have a lot of dosh so maybe stick to the Travel Lodge as they are slightly cheaper.

He booked himself a room for three nights, dumped the small amount of possessions he still had and went off in search of some victims who were stupid enough to let him steal from them to line his pockets. He also realised he had very few clothes now after dumping evidence clothing in dumpsters and losing his bigger holdall. The holdall he was using was torn and needed to be replaced. Feeling very upbeat he headed off to the Reading town centre for his pickings of the day and to do a bit of shop lifting into the bargain.

His first stop was his favourite haunt "Primark". It had never let him down in the past. Today was no exception, he exited the store with a wallet and five purses. He had also managed to steal a pair of jogging pants and a sweater, some underwear and strangely had managed to acquire a store bag in which to carry them. He had a moment of slight panic as he got to the exit with his spoils as a rather huge security guard started to approach him. For a moment a flash of panic shot through him but passed as soon as he realised that the guy was actually racing to help a customer get her buggy through the door.

He smiled as he got out onto the street, "I am invincible" he smugly said to himself, "I can do anything and nobody can catch me !!!"

His next stop was Sports Direct. He came out with a track suit, some tee shirts and a pair of pretty decent trainers. He actually bought the trainers though as they were security tagged and he needed to try them on, but all in all a pretty good morning's work.

He moved on to a camping shop to get a new holdall but ended up paying for it as the store assistant followed him like a puppy dog, so just for badness while he was tilling up his payment *Simon* lifted a rather nice sport watch from the display cabinet.

Feeling great he headed off to the local Wetherspoon for some lunch. After all, all this thieving made a man hungry. Thinking this made him chuckle to himself .

He found a table in a quiet corner. The lunch time rush hadn't yet begun as it was only just after twelve. He ordered a bowl of soup, some bread and a pint of London Pride and settled himself ready to examine his Primark spoils.

One of the purses had very little, just about twenty pounds but he struck lucky with the second one he examined. It only had a few coins in the zip part and two fivers on the wallet part but there was a sort of secret part behind a photograph of a man holding a baby. He tossed the picture to one side but as he did so a very tiny murmur tried to come forward in his brain. It was Tyler, seeing the baby made him wake up if only for a second.

"Fuck off" *Simon* said quite loudly. It was just as the waitress had arrived at his table with his soup. "Oh I am sorry, I didn't mean you" he quickly said when he saw the look on the poor waitresses face "I was just talking to myself". She placed his soup and bread down and left giving him a strange look as she went. Stupid bitch he thought to himself. "Oh thank you!" he shouted after her in a sarcastic manner. Once she was gone he looked in the purse's secret part and found three fifty pound notes. "This day is getting better and better" he said to nobody in particular. He opened the rest of the purses and gathered together eighty-four pounds then opened the wallet. Two hundred and ten pounds in nice crisp notes.

Simon took the stuff he had stolen from Primark and put it into his new holdall and then put all the purses and the wallet into the used Primark bag ready for dumping. He was so pleased with himself he went to the bar and ordered another London Pride. He walked back to his table with his beer just in time to see a girl, dressed in a tracksuit with cap with a ponytail hanging out of the back of it, probably only about sixteen or so, she was leaning over his holdall. She sudden;y turned and saw *Simon* looking and grabbing the holdall turned to run but *Simon* was too fast for her and managed to leap over a small table in time to grab her ponytail and pull her back. Everyone was watching but nobody said a word or moved to help either the girl or *Simon*. They probably thought he was her father and didn't want to get caught up in any domestic.

Simon pulled the girl by her hair back to his table and pushed her down into the seat beside him. He took the bag from her hand and then, still holding he hair asked her what the hell she was thinking.

"Dunno," she said "Just saw it there an fort I'd nick it"

Simon looked at the girl. She was quite dirty. Her face was dirty, her nails were dirty and she had a smell of urine about her.

"Are you living on the street" he asked

The girl nodded. He released her hair but she didn't attempt to run.

"So what's the craic?" he said

"Ain't nuffing" she said. "I left 'ome cause me step dad kept sneaking in me bed an I didn't like it, me mum didn't believe me so I left"

"How long ago" he asked

"'bout a week now"

"So where are you sleeping"

"Ere an there"

"Are you hungry?"

"Yeah I'm starvin" she said and her face lit up with hope in her eyes, thinking maybe this was the break she needed. Somebody to look after her.

Boy was she on the wrong wave length.

Simon took her to the bar and let her order whatever she fancied to eat and a cola drink as he wasn't sure just how old she was. He bought himself a large whisky and they went back to the table.

They chatted for a while and he found out her name was Kelly and although she said she was seventeen he knew she was lying. Then her food arrived. *Simon* was actually beginning to feel a little sorry for the girl, that was until she started eating. She was stuffing her food in like her life depended on it, (unfortunate terminology) it reminded him of Greta in the Indian restaurant back in Bristol and he started to get angry.

"Hurry up and eat your food" he said quite charmingly although feeling quite angry inside "And I'll take you somewhere where you can sleep tonight. I know a few places".

Of course he knew no such thing but he was thinking of the little wooded area he had noticed when he got off the train. Just behind the station. There were a couple of old carriages which had been there for years by the looks of things, and were well overgrown with new growth trees and tall weeds. Perfect, he thought, she will sleep well there...forever.!!!

Simon parked Kelly in a little cafe and ordered her a coke while he went back to his room at the travel lodge and dumped his stuff off.

She was still sitting in the same seat when he got back, stupid trusting bitch he thought to himself. She deserves what's coming for being so stupid.

"Come on then," he called at the door of the cafe. He didn't want to be seen with her just in case some nosy parker recognised him at a later date. Kelly downed the remains of her coke and grabbed her coat as she headed for the door.

Simon started walking towards the station. There were quite a few people about as it was only four O'clock in the afternoon and the schools had emptied so there were gangs of teenagers and little kids with their mums everywhere. *Simon* thought maybe he should wait a while but then just how many people were going to notice them. Even if they did they would probably just think he was a dad with his daughter, nothing unusual in that.

By the time they got to the station the people had thinned out. There were several teenagers waiting to get a train home but they were nearly all on the platforms or kicking the odd football to each other at the entrance. Nobody was interested in *Simon* and Kelly sneaking around the back of the station, crouching down under the weeds and bushes to emerge where two old railway carriages stood decaying in the overgrowth.

One was a passenger carriage with broken windows all along it and the other was a wooden goods carriage. Just one door and no windows. The door was hanging off but you could see that the inside was pretty empty and dry.

"Here ya go" *Simon* said in his nicest voice "your hotel room for the night"

Kelly giggled and climbed into the carriage. *Simon* noticed some old sacks lying in the corner and picked them up and shock them. A few bits of crap fell out and a couple of mice scurried across the floor. This didn't seem to phase Kelly which impressed him as he was sure she would have screamed and run from them as girls so often would. He laid the sacks down on the floor and motioned to Kelly to try them out.

"Not so bad then" he said smiling "And with your coat on top of you you will be quite toasty!" Kelly looked a little hesitant but she did as she was told.

"But it's much too early to go to bed now" she said. "What are we going to do until bed time?"

Simons fist hit her square on the nose which immediately started to bleed profusely, she raised her hand and felt the blood

"What the ..." but she never finished the sentence as a further blow to the top of her head sent her flat out on the sacks.

Simon grinned to himself as he pulled down his tracksuit bottoms and pants and took out his erection. Then, leaning over the girl felt for a pulse, he couldn't find one. He pulled down her tracky bottoms and knickers. Oh my god, he thought as he pulled at them, she was on a period and the mess was horrible. The sanitary towel she had on was sodden in blood and he wanted to be sick. Looking down at his now flaccid penis he pulled up his clothing. Dusted himself off and made for the door leaving the girl lying dead on the pile of rags. He didn't even bother to re dress her or cover her up.

Kelly woke up a couple of hours or so after it happened and didn't know where she was or what had happened but then when she felt the pain in her nose and the dried blood she started to remember. Looking down at the dishevelled clothing she thought for a moment she must have been raped but she wasn't sore although she was in a terrible mess. She hurriedly pulled her clothing back on and put her coat on wrapping it tightly around her and staggered out of the carriage. She scanned the under growth quickly in case her attacker was still about. It was getting dark so she must have been unconscious for hours she thought. All she wanted to do was go home. She was stupid to had rowed with her mother and run away. She had no money and didn't really know what to do. Luckily as she climbed out from the bushes she stumbled and fell, a woman pushing a baby in a buggy caught sight of her and rushed over to help her. Kelly collapsed sobbing into the woman's arms.

Half an hour later she was sitting in a room in the police station, wrapped in a blanket. A police woman had been dispatched to acquire her some dry underwear and sanitary wear and she had on a track suit one of the female officers had spare in their locker . They had taken all Kelly's clothes to examine for traces of the perp.

She had a cup of hot chocolate in front of her and a packet of chocolate hobnobs.

“Right!” the duty sergeant was saying. “As soon as the police constable comes back with some, er, special clothes for you we are taking you to the hospital for a check up, OK?” It wasn't a question.

Kelly nodded just so happy to be alive she didn't care what happened next.

“We have informed your parents and they are on their way, in the mean time do you want to tell us what happened or would you rather wait for them?”

The sergeant was a kind man and Kelly had warmed to him straight away.

“I can tell you everything” she said and proceeded to tell the story.

Apparently she was only fourteen, she had only run away from home two days earlier, after she had rowed with her mother over being told she must be home by 9pm after a friends party and not 11pm which is what she wanted. She had stormed out shouting behind her that she would stay at a friend's. When she hadn't returned by the next morning they were frantic with worry. They had called all her friends' houses with no result so had reported her missing to the police who had been searching for her all that day.

Kelly apologised and asked if they would charge her. The policeman smiled and said it was nothing to worry about, she was safe and that was all that mattered.

Suddenly her parents came rushing into the room and she hugged them both. All the stuff she had told *Simon* had been rubbish. There was no step father creeping into her bed, just a real live dad who worshipped the ground she walked on. She had even put on the awful course accent to make her story seem real. She so much regretted it all now.

Once Kelly was sorted and with her parents heading for the hospital with a police woman the sergeant sat at his computer and scanned for any similar acts of violence that had occurred recently or at least locally. He wasn't sure if the guy had left Kelly for dead or just ran when he didn't get his way but whatever this was a really serious offence and the guy needed to be caught tout de suite.

It didn't take him more than ten minutes to find *Simon* on the list of dangerous people wanted in the south and south-west area of the UK. He immediately sent the picture to his constable who had gone to the hospital with Kelly. The result was that, yes, Kelly confirmed it was a picture of the man who had attacked her.

The sergeant called the policeman leading the investigation.

Toby picked up the call on the first ring and listened as the sergeant told him all about the attack on Kelly.

"Well I am currently in Bristol working on the last attack " Toby said "Same train route out of here as from Cardiff to Bristol and now to Reading...It's our man alright. He must have run after killing Greta. We're on our way!" and with that he looked up at Oliver...."He's in Reading, lets go!"

Within two hours Toby and Oliver were sitting at the bedside of Kelly. The hospital had advised she stay just for one night so they could keep an eye on her as she had a nasty bump on her head although she said she felt fine. Kelly retold her story to them. Toby felt a shudder going down his spine as she spoke. He wanted to tell her just how lucky she was but held back. The kid was so young, but as gently as possible he tried to make her understand that she must be far more careful with strangers. She surprised him by saying that she wasn't as naive as everyone thinks she is and OK she was a bit of an idiot going with *Simon* but he was very convincing about knowing where she could go to sleep for the night and she was so mad at her parents she just wanted to get back at them. She realised now how stupid she had been and that she was never going to do anything quite like that again, she had definitely learned her lesson. At that moment her parents came into the room and by the look on all their faces Toby thought that they had all learned a lesson.

"Right" Oliver said as soon as they were outside and heading for their car. "What's the next move ?"

"Well we have his picture, we know he is in Reading, or was last night anyway, I suggest we start with all the places he could stay. He stayed at a Travel Lodge last time so as good a place to start as any eh?" Toby said. "Can you give the sergeant a call and ask if he can let us have a few officers to help out with our search? Also, get him to inform the press. We can do with all the help we can get. They can release the picture and maybe the public can do some of our search for us."

Toby drove and Oliver made the call as they drove to the centre of Reading and parked up.

CHAPTER 19

Once *Simon* had left Kelly for dead he had raced back to his room only stopping en-route to purchase a decent bottle of scotch. Once there he went into the shower and stood for ages washing the thoughts of what he had seen from his mind and cleansing his body.

He felt tons better after his shower. It was all her fault he told himself. She had spoiled his fun and deserved what happened to her. He didn't consider for one second that even if she had been clean he was going to kill her anyway.

Sitting on the bed and having poured himself a large glass of scotch he relaxed. Put on the TV and even though it was still only afternoon, leaned back and closed his eyes... just for a moment he thought.

When he woke up a few hours later it was dark outside, he checked his watch and realised he was going to be very late for his meeting with the two idiot girls he had met earlier that day, so he decided not to bother. Just poured himself another drink and tuned the TV into some old film that had just started. His attempt to rape Kelly had rather dampened his libido anyway. "Never mind" he thought, "there will be plenty more stupid girls around for me to "play with" - after all tomorrow is another day!" he smiled to himself at the reference he had quoted from a film.

By the time he had finished most of the bottle he was fast asleep.

He woke at around 10.00pm due to some sort of loud talking going on outside his room. Carefully he put his ear to the door. It only took him a few seconds to understand there were policemen outside in the corridor. He heard somebody say his name, well the name he had given the girl on reception when he had registered.

"That looks a bit like a Michael Robins in room 12" she was saying. "I don't know if he is in at the moment though, I'll see if his key is there. Has he done something wrong?"

There was a noise like people walking but then he couldn't hear anything else. Quick as a flash he was packed and climbing out of the window. Luckily his room was on the ground floor or who knows what he would have done.

By the time the police were outside his room and knocking he was gone. Three streets away and mingling with the Friday night revellers.

Now what was he going to do? Before he realised where he was going he was at the bus station. He didn't head for the train station as he thought they must have found Kelly's body and it would be teeming with cops. He had no idea she was actually fine. He did wonder however how they had a picture of him, which they must have by the conversation he had just heard.

That could be a problem, he thought, maybe I will have to change my appearance a little more.

He got on the only bus that had an engine running that looked like it was ready to go. Heading for the back he asked the driver where it was heading, Aldershot was the reply. "Well" thought *Simon* "Full circle" and settled down for the hour long journey.

Not a great time to arrive at a town, almost midnight, but it was a town *Simon* knew really well even though it was years since he had been there. The place had changed hardly at all. He headed straight to the cafe where he had met Tina all those years ago. It was still there but was closed. Next door but two was a pub that he also knew pretty well, although it had been updated quite a bit since he was last drinking in there, he ventured inside. It should have been last orders but the landlord still had so many people in there that he was still serving. *Simon*'s head was a bit heavy after the whiskey he had been drinking so he settled for a pint of Guinness and took it to the only spare table where he sat for a few moments. The banter in the pub was good, mainly young people just enjoying themselves. There was a pool table and a dart board at one end although there was only one person close to either. *Simon* got up and walked over to the pool table and asked if the guy fancied a game.

Three games of pool later *Simon* and Richie, his new best friend, were sitting chatting. Mainly about how Richie was so good at pool that he had beaten *Simon* three games on the trot. Richie was a guy that liked the sound of his own voice and successes, *Simon* had noticed. Still he might be useful for a place to stay he had thought so he put up with the guy's bragging.

It was almost 1am before the landlord told them all to piss off as he wanted to close up and go to bed. Slowly the remaining customers strolled and staggered out through the door leaving *Simon* and Richie still sitting there.

"Aw common now guys" the landlord said "Haven't you got no homes to go to?"

Richie looked at *Simon* "We'd better go now mate" he said "Where are you staying?" *Simon* had told him he had only just arrived in Aldershot but that he had lived there many years before.

"Dunno" *Simon* said. "I was going to find a travel lodge or something but seem to have lost the time chatting with you as you are so interesting" This made Richie feel important and he almost puffed out his chest.

"You can stay at my place if you like" he said. "It's only ten minutes walk from here."

Simon smiled inside, what a prick and so gullible. "Are you sure?" *Simon* put on his most friendly voice. "That would be great if you are sure!"

They left the pub and headed towards the station. Richie lived in a tiny terraced house the other side of the train tracks so they crossed over on the bridge and down the other side. By this time *Simon* had learned that Richie wasn't such a bad guy after all. He was divorced and had three kids whom he adored. He had bought his tiny house after his divorce, mainly so he would have somewhere for his kids to stay on their visits. His wife had moved in with her new man and they had bought a house down in Devon so he only saw the children during school holidays, but was hoping it would all change once they were old enough to visit by themselves.

Hearing this *Simon* felt Tyler start to bristle in his head. He knew that when ever children were mentioned Tyler would try and struggle back into his thoughts.

"Fuck off!" he shouted to his head.

Luckily Richie was a little in front and didn't hear exactly what he said.

"What was that?" he asked innocently turning to hear what *Simon* had said.

"Oh nothing" he said "I was just thinking aloud. He was a little disturbed though as Tyler's struggle to get free was stronger than usual.

As soon as they got into Richie's front room *Simon* collapsed onto one of the easy chairs. He fell asleep in the time it took Richie to go into the kitchen and put the kettle on for coffee.

Richie came back into the lounge asking how *Simon* wanted his coffee and smiled when he saw him sparked out. Richie was a nice man and a kind man. He had felt a little sorry for *Simon* having nowhere to sleep that night, he had been in a similar position on more than one occasion himself. He went upstairs and took a duvet off his spare bed which he brought down and covered *Simon* with. He didn't bother to wake him as it was really late and they had drunk more that their fair share of booze. *Simon* looked quite content so Richie turned off the kettle, put out the lights and went to bed himself. He had no idea just what a monster he was feeling sorry for. If he had known maybe he might have been a little more careful.

The next morning when Richie had showered and dressed he went downstairs to find *Simon* in exactly the same position he was in the previous night and still sparked out. Smiling to himself he wrote a note saying he was off to work but would be home later and that *Simon* was to help himself to breakfast and whatever and that he was welcome to stay another night if he wanted. Richie said he'd be home around 6.00pm. He then propped the note up against a lamp next to the chair and went off to work.

Simon woke and looked at his watch, it read 11.35. His head was banging a version of the 1812 overture so he got out of the chair in search of some sort of pain relief. Seeing Richie's note he smiled. He was warming to the guy which was really unusual for him. He thought yes, he might just stay another night or even longer, you never know.

He found a jar of instant coffee and a packet of paracetamol in one of the kitchen cupboards and while he was boiling the kettle for the coffee he made himself a piece of toast. Once he was settled with his breakfast he started to think of what his next plan was going to be. He had no real idea of just what he wanted to do but he knew he couldn't stay anywhere too long in case the police were looking for him. He assumed they were looking for the killer of Kelly but wasn't too concerned as they probably couldn't link him and they had no idea what he looked like.

How wrong he was. He had no idea Kelly was still alive and had recognised a picture of him. He had no idea that the main policeman searching for him was actually Tilly's husband.

After he finished his toast he carried his coffee mug and went for a nose around Richie's house.

He opened all the drawers he came across in the dining room but found nothing of any interest so he ventured into the lounge, picked up the duvet he had left on the floor by the chair he had slept in and folded it neatly and placed it back onto the chair. Then turning to the table with the lamp where he had seen the note propped he noticed there was a silver picture frame with a picture of three little smiling boys, probably aged between 2 and 5 he thought. Suddenly his head started to spin, Tyler was fighting to get free. Fuck off! Fuck off! *Simon* was screaming now and banging the front of his head with the flat of his hand. Tyler had never felt so strong. *Simon* was the boss, *Simon* was in control but at this moment in time he wasn't !!! It only lasted for about a minute or so but then *Simons* head just stared to ache violently and Tyler was gone.

He moved back into the lounge and sat in the chair he had spent the night in and put his head in his hands to try and stop the pounding going on in his head. It was a complete reverse of the norm as it was Tyler who used to have the headaches when *Simon* was waking up but now *Simon* was worried that Tyler was getting stronger again.

It was at least an hour before his headache subsided, by which time he had convinced himself that it was just his hangover that had caused it. But just in case, he turned the picture of Richie's boys face down so he couldn't see them.

He needed a plan of action. He was weighing up whether to hang on here with Richie for a while, after all it wasn't going to cost him too much, or move on. He knew he would have to steal some money from somewhere as he had very little left from his last stealing spree.

He wondered around the rest of Richie's little house. Opening drawers and cupboards in all the rooms upstairs. Nothing much to see until he came across a shoe box at the bottom of one of the boys wardrobes. He at first thought it would just contain some of their toys but on closer inspection realised there was another smaller plastic box inside. Intrigued he removed the lid and there inside was a folded padded envelope containing a money clip. *Simon* could hardly believe his eyes. What a bloody stupid and obvious place to hide money, I mean a bloody shoe box at the bottom of a wardrobe, just how 'Alfred Hitchcock movie' was that? Then he thought perhaps he had just popped it there as he knew *Simon* would be alone in his house. This made him cross, he didn't bloody trust me eh? Now he found it easy to make up his mind, take the money and run. He took the money out of the clip and laid it on the bed, seventeen thousand pounds in fifties, a few tenners and a couple of fivers too. Your lucky day old chap, he said to himself stuffing the money onto his pocket. It never occurred to him that maybe it had always been kept there. He just wanted a reason to hate Richie so he would have an excuse in his head to take the money and run.

He put the box back in the wardrobe. Went downstairs and on a scrap of paper he found in the kitchen he scribbled a note saying he was thankful for the help, he smiled to himself as he wrote that as he meant it in both ways, help in giving him a bed for the night and help in giving him all that cash. Although Richie wouldn't know that until he went to check his box, and that could be days, weeks or months away...or hours !!!

He said he would be in touch but knew he never would.

It was almost 6.30pm when Richie arrived home, he went straight into the kitchen and put the kettle on. He called *Simon*, almost expecting to find him still asleep in the lounge but when he had no reply he wondered through the house looking to see if he was actually still around.

He had to admit to himself that it was a bit of a relief to find the house empty. He thought *Simon* was OK but there was something in his eyes that worried Richie, he didn't know why but he felt he wouldn't like to trust him too much. At this thought he remembered his box upstairs. Unlike what *Simon* had thought, Richie hadn't stashed it away out of his guest's eyes. He always kept it in his son's bedroom wardrobe. It was the money he had kept after the sale of his marital home and was hoping one day, when the children were older to take them on a journey of a lifetime to maybe Australia or America, hiring a Winnebago and spending at least a month with them. Just thinking of this made him excited although he knew it was not going to happen for a few years yet.

As soon as he went into his son's bedroom he knew what he was going to find. The wardrobe door was ajar when it never is and the bed had been sat on he could tell. His heart was pounding as he dared to look in the shoe box. As his heart sank lower and lower into his body tears started to break though his eyes and trickle down his cheeks. “What a stupid fool you are Richie” he said to himself, “how could you have been such an idiot?”

He sat there with the empty envelope in his hand and cried.

While this was happening in Aldershot *Simon* was on a train heading for Guildford having kitted himself out with some new clothes and had his hair cut and highlighted so he looked very different, just in case. He had been growing a beard when he attacked Kelly but was clean shaven now, again just in case.

When Richie had pulled himself together he decided he was going to the police to report the theft. He assumed they wouldn't be able to do anything but it would make him feel better. He was seething inside and beating himself up for being so bloody stupid.

He walked into town and headed towards the police station, passing the newspaper seller sitting outside the station. On the side of his kiosk was the headline of the evening edition. He stopped as soon as he saw it. “Have you seen this man?” it said and there was a picture of *Simon.* He bought a paper and stood while he read the details of how the man was wanted in connection with several attacks. It didn't give too much detail of his crimes, just that the police were very keen to interview him.

Richie increased his pace toward the police station once he had read this. All he could think of was bastard, bastard, bastard!

He arrived at Aldershot police station and explained everything to the policeman on the front desk and waved the newspaper at the man showing him exactly who he was talking about. Almost instantly the astute constable was on the computer checking about the man in the picture as he had heard they were searching in Reading for the man but Aldershot was only a bus ride away.

Within an hour Toby and Oliver were in the interview room at Aldershot police station with Richie sitting opposite them, all with Costa cups of coffee in front of them.

Excitement was washing over Toby as he asked the man if he would like to tell them all he knew. Richie was quite ready for that as he was so very angry with *Simon* taking him for a chump and stealing his money.

At the end of his statement he asked just what *Simon* was wanted for. He assumed he had stolen from others and maybe he had attacked somebody during a theft.

Although Toby wanted to tell this guy just how lucky he had been just to get away with a theft and nothing worse, and to tell him just how dangerous *Simon* was, he held back. After all, until they knew that he was actually the same man who did all the murders and attacks they had to keep quiet. He just told Richie that there were a few outstanding issues they needed to interview the man about and now there was a new issue, meaning the theft Richie had just reported.

Richie seemed reasonably content with this explanation and said he would be around if they needed him for any identification parades or anything. At this statement Oliver smiled inwardly as he was thinking "somebody's been watching Frost or similar on the TV" but he obviously said nothing.

Toby on the other hand was still a little worried that maybe *Simon* would return to Richie's for whatever reason so as Richie was at the door he said "Maybe if you see *Simon* you could let us know straight away and don't let him into your house or go near him. OK ?"

At this Richie turned and said "You can be sure that if I see that bastard anywhere near me or my house again I'll kill him!"

Toby just nodded as if to say, I totally understand mate but added "Not that wise really mate, just call us if you see him please"

It wasn't long before the posse Toby had sent out to check Reading town came back with a positive sighting.

The call from Reading was patched through to the Aldershot station.

They had two confirmed sightings, one of the posse members told Toby, and had statements from both people concerned. One, a waitress who worked in Wetherspoon's had said she had served him and that she thought he was a bit strange as he had been swearing at himself, and the other was the receptionist at one of the Travel Lodges. He told Toby that when they had originally been there the receptionist had said it might be a guy who had checked into room 31 but it had been locked when they visited it, then when they took a second visit to the room a few minutes later after checking the other rooms and locating the key to 31 it was empty. They think he must have heard them outside his door the first time and climbed out of the window. The receptionist said he had booked for three days and as this was only one day in they were convinced it was him.

They had checked around the streets and cafes but no sign so they went to the train and bus stations. Before he said any more Toby stopped him, he's in Aldershot, he said, or rather he was. We have no idea if he still is .

"That would make sense" the guy the other end said, the bus station had recorded a bus leaving for Aldershot that evening.

CHAPTER 20

Once *Simon* had left Richie's house he headed to the greasy spoon cafe and filled his stomach with a nice greasy fry and two more mugs of coffee and started to feel human again. The paracetamol had done their duty and the fry had just topped up his mood. Right, he thought, where to next? Probably best to get out of Aldershot just in case Richie did check his shoe box and came looking for him. Maybe he should get himself a cheap car, after all he had the money now.

He asked the guy at the counter if he had a local paper anywhere around and the guy lifted his head from his phone for a second pointed to the end of the counter where there was a paper rack that *Simon* hadn't noticed.

“Might be one in there” he said with little interest and turned his eyes straight back to his phone.

“Ignorant git” *Simon* thought to himself, if I was going to hang around I might just have had to take him down a peg or two.

He found loads of cheap cars for sale so he selected the youngest of the cheapest and headed for the phone box to call the seller, then he suddenly thought why don't I buy a phone, stupid sod. Are there still phone boxes anyway? He headed to the closest phone shop and bought a pay as you go phone. He was going to go for the cheapest at first as he was so used to going that way but hey a light bulb moment suddenly hit him, he had cash now, quite a bit , so why not go for something good for a change?

Feeling smug and almost happy he headed to a pub where he bought a beer, as it was almost mid day, and settled with the paper he had taken from the cafe and phoned the number for the car he had selected. It was sold, so he went through the ads again and selected a second, again sold. He was on his second beer before he found one that was still available. He got directions of where to go to try it out, got a cab from outside the train station and gave the address to the cab driver.

Half an hour later he was driving an old style black VW golf thinking to himself what a good job Tina had taught him to drive all those years ago.

The car had belonged to a boy racer by the looks of things as it had bright red flames painted on the front wings and flared arches. *Simon* actually thought it was great fun. He had only paid 950 pounds for it, he had bartered it down from 1100 so he was really chuffed. Apparently it had belonged to the son of the woman he bought it from, but the son had "gone away" she had told him. He suspected it was to prison but didn't ask.

Where to go was his next thought but before he had even started to consider this he found himself driving along the Hogs Back towards Guildford.

Once he arrived in Guildford he found himself heading straight to the road he had lived in when he was with Sam. He had no idea at first why he ended up there but then suddenly he knew.

His head stared to hurt like it had never hurt before. He had to pull the car to the side of the road as he could hardly see through the pain. Tyler had broken free.

Fuck off! Fuck off! *Simon* screamed out but Tyler was pushing harder and harder to take over his brain.

I need to see Sam, I need to see Dylan, I need to see my new baby.

NO! NO! *Simon* was shouting now, get back I don't need you here. He didn't realise he was banging his head against the inside of the drivers window until some passers by tapped on the window and mouthed was he OK? Suddenly Tyler fell back and *Simon's* strength came to the fore. He wound down the window and smiled at the concerned couple looking in at him.

"Sorry," he said, " I was listening to a really good rock song and got a bit carried away!"

They both smiled and walked off. Although when they got out of sight they both looked at each other and burst out laughing.

"There was no radio noise coming from that car", the man said. "I think he was just a nutter!" The girl with him nodded and they went on their way.

Simon stayed in the same spot for a while longer. He had fought Tyler with all his strength but wasn't sure if he had won. The pull to his life with Sam and the babies was getting stronger and stronger. He should never have come back to Guildford but it was Tyler who had brought him here. He must get away, he thought, somewhere miles away.

He started the car and headed out of town and towards London.

At the same time he was doing this the couple who had tapped on his window had gone into the nearest pub for some lunch. The guy, Steve, went to the bar to order while Jo, his girlfriend, settled at a table. She casually picked up a national newspaper that somebody had left on the seat. There on the front page was a picture of the guy they had just seen.

OK it wasn't an exact match but very close. She began to read the narrative under the picture and went cold.

"Steve, quick come here!" she called to him.

Steve turned with the drinks in his hand and was shocked by the look on his girlfriends face. Hurriedly he crossed the room.

"What's wrong Jo?"

Jo pushed the paper in front of him, "Wanted in connection with assaults, and it says he could be dangerous!"

"OK don't freak, he's not here. I think we should tell the police though." Steve took out his phone and called 999. He knew it wasn't exactly an emergence but thought it would be the quickest way to get through to the local police station. The response on the phone wasn't what he had expected, the woman at the end of the line did have a go at him for dialling the emergency service but once he explained she put him straight through to Guildford police station.

Simon got five miles or so out of Guildford before the pain in his head started to erupt again. It was so bad that he almost lost his vision. He had to pull off the main road and into a field entrance where he parked the car and got out to try and clear his head.

Tyler was angry because they were heading out of Guildford. He was desperate to see Sam and Dylan and also see his new baby. He had no recollection of what *Simon* had done. How he had beaten Sam and killed her father. That was how it worked in *Simon's* head. It was totally split into two people. Tyler the guy struggling to have a normal life and *Simon*, originally created to be Tyler's protector, had grown so strong he had taken over almost all of the time now. For the past year it had just been *Simon*, pushing Tyler out and until recently Tyler had only been a little annoyance, who *Simon* could shut down, but seeing the pictures of Richie's boys had woken Tyler and arriving in Guildford had made him even stronger. When Tyler was normal he loved Sam and his son and was really looking forward to his new baby's birth until *Simon* had taken over, he didn't like Tyler being so soft.

While *Simon* was up to the madness he carried out on Sam and her father, Tyler had been put to the back of his brain. Although Tyler was vaguely aware of what *Simon* was doing there was nothing he could do to stop him so he had just gone back to sleep.

He was the weak part of his brain now. Having created *Simon* to help him when he was being assaulted as a child, *he* had been his saviour but as his life had progressed *Simon* had not been quite so necessary. He had tried to shut *him* out of his head but *he* had grown too strong and now was almost in total control.

Tyler's yearning for his wife and babies was growing and he was fighting with *Simon* to gain control back. He had no idea that if he was to go to Sam's the outcome would be devastating for both him and *Simon* as obviously the police did not know there were in fact two people in one brain.

He was struggling to smother *Simon* but wasn't succeeding. *Simon* was determined to keep control. He popped three paracetamol in his mouth and chewed until they were gone, they tasted like poison but he had to get rid of this headache before he could drive on.

Twenty minutes later he was back on the road. His head still hurt but not quite as bad. At least he could see straight now. He followed the main drag until he came to a little village with a name sign as you entered. Hares End. He thought of a hare and thought of its end and it cheered him up. Maybe somebody had found a hare once and shot it, or better still wrung its neck, these were the sort of thoughts that made *Simon* smile to himself. They would have taken it into the village and thrown it onto the green, and when the people came to see it he would announce that it was the Hares End and that was how the village got it's name. Of course that was probably a load of old tosh but *Simon* chose to think it could be true.

He parked outside the only pub and went in. His headache was easing by the second so he felt he deserved a beer or two. He ordered a pint of the guest ale and a ham and cheese toasty and picking up the daily paper from the rack by the bar went and sat at a table in the far corner where he was almost hidden from any prying eyes.

There, on the front page he saw himself staring back at him. OK his hair was now shorter and the designer stubble had gone but there was no mistaking it was himself.

Slipping a little lower into the seat, as if that would make any difference, he fished around in his holdall and pulled out a cap he had stolen on one of his Primark expeditions, thinking at the time that it was so naff he just had to have it. It had writing on the front which read "My other cap is a Nike." He put it on and pulled it low at the front. Then hid his head in the middle of the newspaper just as his sandwich arrived. He needn't have worried, he thought, as the girl who brought it over didn't even glance at him, just plonked it down on the table with a small basket full of various sauces and mustards and walked away.

The girl hurried back to the bar and nudged the barman as she passed, inclining her head for him to follow her out to the kitchen.

Once safely out of earshot of the bar she nodded to Tony the barman.

"It's is him definitely" she said. "Are you going to call the police?"

"Are you absolutely sure?" Tony said "I don't want to call them and then it not be him!"

"Well you thought it was too!" Dianne said. "I only glanced but I am sure you are right."

"Well let's just see if he comes back for another beer and then we can both look just to make sure"

By the time they had finished discussing this *Simon* had eaten his toastie, finished his beer and was three miles down the road in his Golf.

Dianne went out to the bar but before she reached his table she could see that he was gone. Rushing back to Tony she told him to call the police anyway as she was sure it must have been him as he had disappeared so quickly and the newspaper was left on his table with the picture of him staring up at her.

Tony did as he was instructed, although "shutting the stable door after the horse has bolted" was the phrase that sprang to mind as he did so.

Bloody newspapers, *Simon* thought to himself as he was driving. Trying to think of a way he could disguise himself so he didn't have to go undercover. Eventually, about twenty or so miles later he had come up with the only thing he could.

He was near Dorking by this time but avoided the town as he remembered from years before that it was an expensive place to stay, so instead he headed for Horsham and then on to Crawley. There was a Holiday inn just outside the town but before he booked himself in he went to a local Spar shop where he purchased a razor and some shaving foam. He had his cap pulled firmly down over his face and a hoodie on so the only looks he got were from people who looked a little anxious thinking he might be a thug or pull a knife so nobody came anywhere near him. Even the shop girl just took his money and moved away after she had given him his change.

Simon then had to look more normal when he went into the Holiday Inn or they might had refused him a room. He got a scarf out of his holdall and tied it around his mouth and part of his nose. He then went up to the reception and in a muffled voice asked for a room, explaining that he had just been to the dentist and had been told to keep his mouth warm as he had had three extractions.

The receptionist showed sympathy and prattled on about that she had had the same and knew how sore it could be. *Simon* couldn't give a rats arse about her problem but he nodded and grunted a bit. She gave him the key to room 301. He was just walking away when she called him back.

For a second he felt panic but all she wanted was to offer him some Aspirin in case his pain got too bad. He took the strip of five she gave him, nodded a thanks and headed to the lift.

Once in room 301 he breathed a sigh of relief and immediately opened the mini bar and removed a miniature whiskey that looked as if it was waiting for him there. Once downed he proceeded with his plan.

Half an hour later he emerged from the bathroom with a completely shaved head. He looked in the mirror and was actually impressed with what he saw. "You know *Simon*" he said to himself " You look pretty good shaved" then he chuckled and opened the mini fridge again, and happy to find there was a second miniature whiskey, albeit a different type but good enough.

He settled, propped up on the bed with his drink , and started to try and form the next stage of the plan.

He knew he had to get away from the area, and even the country might be a better bet, but where? He had a passport but he didn't look anything like the picture on it now and of course there might be an astute airline security officer who might recognise the passport or even maybe there might be a control on the system to check for him. He had no idea.

So he needed to go somewhere that didn't need a passport or too much of a check. Immediately Ireland came to mind but then the thought of driving down to Wales and then booking a ferry risking he might be recognised, even with his shaved head, there was still a small risk. No it would have to be nearer to home but somewhere nobody would be that interested in the English papers...Scotland would be the perfect choice he thought, as far up as he could go. He would sit tight up there for a few months until he was forgotten about and grow his hair again and a beard. Yes he would become a hippy and blend into the crowd again. Then he could get on with what ever he wanted. That thought made him start to yearn for some excitement. Maybe another murder. He licked the whiskey off his lips at the thought. Yes maybe a boy again, he had rather enjoyed that little episode in his life and that was ages ago.

He pulled out a map that he had in his holdall and laid it in his lap but as he did so a small pain started again in his head. “You are not coming out!” he shouted to Tyler.

CHAPTER 21

Toby was passed the details of the call that had been received from the Guildford police and together Oliver and he were back in their car and heading into Guildford town to chat with the couple who had made the call.

They took the statement from the couple and then thanked them. Once outside the station they looked at one another.

"Where to now then?" they said in unison.

"Not a bloody clue" Toby said. "I doubt he is still around here, although could he actually have the nerve to go to his old address?" He had only been about a street away when the couple they had just interviewed had seen him.

They knew that Sam and her babies were safe as they had moved after Sam's dad had been killed. They were now safe and well in Devon and there was no way Tyler/*Simon* could have found out where they were. But just to be on the safe side they went to his old address to check he wasn't around.

The people who now lived in the house where Sam had lived were completely surprised to get a visit from the police. They had no knowledge of anybody called Tyler or *Simon.* They had heard rumours that there had been an incident in the house but didn't know too many details.

Oliver thanked them and went back to join Toby in the car.

"No joy, they haven't seen anybody lurking around or knocking on the door, which in one way is a good thing for them anyway, although we are back to square one I reckon"

"Well I think we should call the station and get a message to Sam just in case he has managed to trace her. I'll tell them to send a family liaison officer and not to frighten her with a uniform knocking on her door."

"Now how about getting something to eat and we can have a think while we're eating? I'm starving and I can't remember the last time we ate, can you?" Toby said.

They headed to the nearest pub and while Oliver settled at a table and ordered two roasts of the day dinners when the waitress came over, Toby went to the bar and ordered two pints of bitter shandy.

Once they had satisfied the hunger pangs a little Toby got out his note book and started to list all the places they had been while chasing *Simon.*

OK let's go right back to Sam and her family first, here in Guildford.

Toby had always been convinced that there must be a pattern in *Simon's* movements and he thought that maybe the guy had a plan but the way he had been going back and forth in the last few months it seemed that he had been wrong. There wasn't an end goal, but he did seem to like this area. Maybe he thought as he knew it so well he felt safer.

They had wondered several times if he would try and contact Sam, even if just to see if the baby was alright but they had decided he was such an animal that he didn't even care. He must have known he had killed Sam's dad and maybe even Sam and her unborn baby. Toby wondered just what sort of monster he was and then he realised he was talking about the same monster that did what he did to his beloved Tilly and his best friend Mike.

“I think we should go back to the station and start to list everything again” Oliver said. “We have to catch him before he attacks or even kills again. I expect now his picture has been out there he will have to lie low for a while at least. He'll probably change his looks as much as possible, probably with a beard or shave his head or buy some glasses. He will have to be very careful as people are really good at recognising wanted people once their picture is on the TV or national papers. Although he is not headline news I know they will have put his picture up on the local TV stations.”

“Maybe we should just have a drive around say fifty miles of here and check out the hotels, he seems to favour the Travel Lodges so we should start there” Toby said.

They both took out their phones and went on line searching for Travel Lodges in a fifty mile radius of Guildford, thirty seven appeared.

“Wow I didn't realise there were so many of them” Oliver said as he scrolled though the addresses. “It's a shame we only have the one car, maybe you should drop me back and I'll get my car. It'll be faster in the long run.”

“Good shout” Toby said, “but as we are already 20 miles past the station I think we might as well carry on. I'll call the station and get them to send a couple of PC's out on the roads north and west of here and we'll take the south and east. If he is worried about being spotted he might just have grabbed the first place he could get to and lay low.”

Then a call came through of the possible sighting at Hares end.

They noted the Travel Lodges within striking distance of that village and headed east towards the pub of the sighting.

When they arrived at the pub both Tony and Dianne explained that they were pretty sure it was him but not totally convinced.

“Sounds like a good shout to me!” Toby said as they headed out to their car, “It was in the right direction anyway, lets carry on. I have a good feel about this one”

Six Travel lodges later and with still no no luck Oliver noticed a sign for a Holiday Inn just off the road on the left and turning to Toby said “Worth a try, I reckon?”

They pulled up outside.

They got out and stretched. Overlooked by room 301 !!!!

Simon went cold, he recognised that they were coppers easily, even thought neither of them was in any type of uniform and neither seemed to have extra large feet !

Obviously *Simon* wasn't sure but he suspected. So what, he thought to himself, they will never recognise me now. Thinking that, he looked at himself in the mirror.....yep they would never recognise him.

The guys walked into the reception and towards the girl sitting behind a switchboard at the end of the counter.

She stood almost immediately when she heard the automatic doors slide open and put on her “receptionist smile” just as they approached.

“How may I help you gentleman. Is it one room or two?”

This made both Oliver and Toby smile inwardly, bless her she was being tactful they both thought at the same time.

“Not a room thank you miss” Toby began and introduced himself and Oliver, as Oliver produced the picture of *Simon.*

“Have you seen this man at all, maybe he booked in here?“

The receptionist took the picture and looked for a long minute.

“Well I don't think so”, she said and was just about to hand it back when she suddenly did a double take. “although...” and she looked again. “He does look familiar. A guy came in a few hours ago but he had a hat pulled down covering a bit of his face and a scarf around his mouth as he said he had just come from the dentist, but when he pulled it down a little to speak I could see a bit more of his face. Now I can't be absolutely sure but I think it might be him.”

Toby and Oliver looked at each other.

“Is he still in his room” Toby almost dared not to ask .

“Well I did have a half-hour break an hour or so ago when he might have gone out but other than that I personally haven't seen him leave.”

“Who would have been on reception while you were on a break?” Toby said. “Could we speak with the person please?”

“Oh it was Alicia, I'll get her for you”

Two minutes later the girl came back. “I have spoken to Alicia and she said that only one person went through reception while I was out and that was old Mr Flaggerty, he spoke to her so she is sure it was him. So your man must still be in his room, it is 301“ the girl said, feeling quite proud that she had helped.

All the time this was going on downstairs *Simon* was preparing himself to do a disappearing act.

He was convinced that the girl on reception would not have recognised him and even more so now he had shaved his head and he wasn't absolutely that the men he had seen coming into the hotel were in fact the police, so he wasn't overly concerned, but did think it would be wise to make a quick exit just in case. He wouldn't be able to take everything if he was just going to slip out through the fire escape pronto so he just put on his hoody and wrapped the scarf around his face and was gone before Toby and Oliver had even got to the second floor.

They stood, one each side of the door and knocked. Nothing, knocked again, nothing.

"Do you think he is asleep" Oliver whispered "or saw us come in? Could he have guessed we were police?"

Oliver ran downstairs and got the hotel key from the girl on reception. She was a little hesitant at first until Oliver told her why they were after the guy.

The room was of course empty but once inside they were careful not to disturb anything as they didn't want him thinking they were on to him.

"He must have seen us and gone out of the fire escape" Toby said. "But he has left his belongings so I would reckon he legged it just in case... I bet he is so convinced the girl downstairs didn't recognise him and we are just a couple of cops who would just try the door and then come back later if necessary. He will probably come back later for his stuff if he sees us leave, oh and when he does............"

They went back downstairs and said goodbye to the girl saying they would keep hold of the key to room 301 for a little longer just in case they need to get in.

Once outside they made a pretence in the car of shrugging and pretending to call in that they had had no luck. All this just in case *Simon* was watching.

Then they got into the car and drove off.

Simon heard all this from behind one of the dumpsters in the corner of the car park.

"Stupid morons" he said to himself. "They will never catch me."

He waited twenty minutes just to ensure the morons had actually gone and then crept back up the fire escape and back to room 301. Luckily he had left his cap in the lock on the fire door so it could be opened from the outside. Another pat on the back to himself. He smiled as he went into his room.

Toby and Oliver were two miles up the road and on the phone to the station. They requested one female and one male officer to dress as tourists and arrive as a couple to the Hotel as soon as possible, book in and act naturally. Then watch and wait until *Simon* is spotted, preferably outside the hotel as they didn't want any situations where a member of the public might get hurt.

They ordered three unmarked backup cars to be positioned on the three roads surrounding the hotel with at least four policemen inside ready to chase in case of him running.

Lizzy and Duncan changed from their police uniforms and used Lizzy's old car to drive to the Holiday Inn. They smiled at the girl on reception and booked a double room for three nights. She gave them room 304 which was handy as was opposite 301. They didn't let the girl know who they were so it was just a fluke they got a well- positioned room.

Toby had phoned the girl on reception and told her that they would be watching the hotel from down the road so not to worry about anything but to call Toby's number if he checked out. He didn't give too much detail just in case she got worried or accidentality gave the suspect a heads up that he was being watched.

It was dark before *Simon* put in an appearance. At 8.00pm he swanned down to the dining room, brazenly passing through reception as he did so. Clare, the girl on reception didn't even notice him to begin with as he was in a bright red casual shirt, not the dark hoodie she had seen him in previously and he had a shaved head. She thought he must be another guest but then how come she hadn't seen him before. Then the penny dropped. She called Toby .

“Do you think he is in the hotel?” she asked. “Because I have just seen somebody walk through to the dining room that I didn't recognise because he has a shaved head and is wearing bright clothes.”

Toby called Lizzy and suggested they go down for dinner and check this guy out. They both knew exactly what *Simon* looked like having seen his picture so many times, with beard, without beard so he was sure they would recognise him even with a shaved head.

The adrenaline was pumping through Toby's body as he waited for Lizzy to respond.

Affirmative was the word he had been so waiting for.

Toby updated the other officers and then he and Oliver walked into the dining room.

Gone was the hope of getting him outside, this was too good a chance as he was just sitting at a table with a glass of whiskey in front of him.

Lizzy and Duncan were being shown to their table but as they passed *Simon* Duncan grabbed him tightly on the arm by which time Oliver and Toby were there with the cuffs ready and that was almost an anti climax. They had him, they couldn't believe it. Suddenly *Simon* swung around and smashed his whiskey glass at whoever was the closest. This happened to be Oliver who just caught the edge of the glass on his chin. Blood splattered everywhere and people started to shout but Toby had him, no way was this bastard ever getting away.

In the end it took all four of them to drag *Simon* outside to a waiting police car with him protesting his innocence for whatever they were arresting him for. It took every ounce of Toby's strength not to get him on the floor and smother him then and there.

Oliver grabbed Toby's arm and shook his head as he knew exactly what was going through his mind at the time.

"Take him to the station" Oliver instructed the men "and keep him cuffed he is a very dangerous man. Now come on Toby take me to A&E so I can get a stitch in this chin before I bleed all over your car. Well done mate" he added

"You too" Toby said "for the other thing too."

They drove to the hospital where Oliver got three stitches and then on to Guildford police station.

Simon was in the cells out of the way for now, all the police in the office were shaking hands with each other and patting Toby and Oliver on the back.

"Let's leave him there to stew while we go and celebrate!" one of the officers said.

"No not yet" Toby said. "We have to question him and charge him before we can celebrate. You guys go off and have a beer or two!"

Once it was quieter both guys just sat there in silence for a few moments then Toby said "I just hope we can prove everything he's done, I want that bastard to go away for life at least three times over!" But was secretly thinking just how was he going to kill him.

Oliver put a hand on Toby's shoulder and said "Don't even think what you are thinking now." He knew of course.

Almost as if by divine intervention, Toby's phone jumped into action.

He took the call.

CHAPTER 22

Susan Peaches was an up and coming PC who was very highly rated at her station in Brighton. Totally expected to rise in the ranks very quickly. She was also known as The Rot, a name she was secretly quite proud of. It was short for Rottweiler as her reputation was that once she got her teeth into something she wouldn't let go.

That had been the case for the past few weeks. Having recently split up with her boyfriend she had needed something to take her mind off the upset and had found researching old unsolved crimes did just that. She had got so obsessed with it and she had spent all her spare moments in the evenings with her laptop looking at newspaper records of any crimes involving violence. She had homed in on quite a few, made copious notes and then once back at the station started to search for all the information she could using the police database where she could access the records in depth. She started checking for patterns or the same name cropping up more than once, but nothing.

In some cases there had been an assault or even a murder but on further investigation there had been no leads and so the files, although remaining open, were almost forgotten about. These were the cases that the Rot really wanted to get her teeth into.

The first was two murders that had happened in Brighton back in the late nineties. A school girl had been found dead on a patch of rough ground near where there had been a school dance the night before. There had been very little intel and no witnesses had come forward. There were several interviews and statements taken from the attendees at the dance but nothing of any help. One lad had said he asked if he could walk her home but she had refused. She had been walking with her friends until they split up and she went off on her own. Apparently they were the last ones to see her. There was never any suspicion that any of them were involved.

Almost two years later there was another murder in the same area. A young student was found dead in an old warehouse behind a pizza place that was frequented by the local college goers. Again no witnesses, As Susan trolled through the pages of anything suspicious that occurred around that time so spotted there was a slightly mysterious death reported but never followed up. It was a woman who apparently fell into a river while searching for her daughter to tell her that her father had had a heart attack. It wasn't considered suspicious in the eyes of the law as there were no assault marks on the body when it was recovered, just bruising that was expected from the river dragging the body down stream but the daughter was adamant that her mother was an extremely good swimmer and would never have drowned. She had insisted that they look for her boyfriend to see if he had witnessed anything but he had moved away. It was never pursued.

Susan looked at this file and the name of the boyfriend was there in black and white. Tyler Murdoch. She quickly scanned back to the first murder of schoolgirl Jenny. She felt she recognised the name Tyler Murdoch from somewhere. Was it there ?

Yes, he was the lad who had offered to walk the poor ill-fated Jenny home. Hmm she thought, did nobody bother to follow that up ?

She carried on searching but no mention of a Tyler Murdoch. But two people dead in the same area in a short time and the same name cropping up. Probably nothing but worth doing a little more digging she thought.

Susan started to think, if, and it is a very big if, this Tyler was connected in some way and he just disappeared where might he have gone ? She started to search bus and train routes from Brighton of which there were loads of course but drawing a huge circle around a thirty mile radius and searching for murders or vicious assaults in those areas just drew a blank. But the Rot being the Rot did not leave it there.

She drew an even bigger radius and an even longer time scale. Up to ten years, up to sixty miles bingo !!!!!

Six and a half years after the death or the woman in the river two unsolved deaths occurred in Southampton. OK she was probably clutching at straws for a possible connection but thought it was worth a stab.

Again no witnesses, very little to go on. The boy had been raped and the girl bludgeoned. It was in the dock area where there was many rent boy scams going on so it was just assumed that somebody didn't want to pay up and was attacked by the partner in crime but had bitten off more that they could chew. In short the police at the time did not show too much interest. Susan could just hear them now, “Serves the buggers right. Probably somebody came off one of the boats for a bit of fun and got shafted, didn't like it and took their revenge!”

The more Susan looked at these crimes the madder she was getting. Why had nobody tried to find justice for these poor souls. It didn't matter what they were up to they didn't deserve to die.

Susan kept on with her searching and came across an assault in Chertsey. A woman had been left tied, beaten and gagged. Although not life threatening it was a nasty assault. Again a name cropped up, Tyler. Could it be the same person or just a coincidence? Susan was beginning to get excited. She knew of course that there were plenty of Tylers around but she had a real feeling that she was on to something.

She trolled through about a dozen more unsolved attacks and one murder but didn't find any type of connection until she found Sam and Sam's dad. Far more recent, only three years ago but very disturbing and in Guildford. The perp had left a pregnant wife kicked and battered and had returned and killed the poor woman's father just as the ambulance had taken the daughter away. The husband's name was Tyler. Bingo Susan thought.

She opened all the recent files on murders of savage attacks and came up with Orla, Rebecca both very badly beaten, in fact Rebecca was left for dead. Then there was a Kelly in Reading. All these seemed to be on the same rail line. Brighton, Chertsey, Guildford, Cardiff, Bristol, Reading all easily accessible on the same line.

Although not a mention of a Tyler but a mention of *Simon.* Could he have changed his name? At first Susan dismissed it all as her wanting it to be the same man but then an up to date wanted poster came up on the screen. He was wanted for numerous attacks and possible murders and more recently for a robbery where the victim had recognised the man as *Simon.*

At this point Susan knew she had the right man. He was Tyler.

She immediately called the number of the detective in charge.

CHAPTER 23

Toby had put Susan on speaker phone so Oliver had heard the conversation. After she had given a brief explanation they asked her to get over to Guildford police station as soon as possible even though it was 9.00pm by this time none of them seemed to care. Susan was as excited as the guys were and was so thrilled they had taken her findings as brilliant detective work and had praised her accordingly.

Once she had hung up the guys looked at each other and even did a high five. What a result. Although now they knew the real work would begin. There appeared to be so much they didn't know about *Simon* or Tyler but they now knew they were definitely the same man and with a really scary history by the sounds of things. Just how many people had he killed or attacked? There was a hell of a lot of investigating to do and they would need their full team to get on it first thing in the morning.

Susan was at Guildford within the hour and once settled with coffee and a KFC bucket in front of the three of them they began to work through the information Susan had collated.

It was well after 1.00am before they sat back and relaxed. Susan had done a wonderful job and they had plenty of new information to investigate further. They had enough confirmed evidence to hold *Simon* while they followed up all of Susan's findings and Toby didn't want to go to the CPS until he had more. He knew they had him on at least one murder charge and several attacks but he wanted more, he wanted to prove everything that the bastard had ever done. He wanted to tell the people he had damaged along the way the he was going to make sure *Simon* never saw the light of day again but more than anything he was thinking of Tilly. She wasn't just a victim he had murdered her by killing her mind. Which was as bad as if he had put a gun to her head and pulled the trigger.

They decided to call it a day at 1.30am with Susan promising to return for the briefing the following morning. Toby said he would arrange it with her DI.

As they walked out to their cars it was apparent that although they were so tired there was a fresh spring in their steps.

Oliver slept like a log that night but not Toby. His mind was on just how he was going to remove *Simon* from the land of the living. Oh he knew he would have to bide his time, wait for the charges to be confirmed and even wait for the trial . He wanted the lives of the people *Simon* had wrecked due to his murderous ways, like Sam's father, Toby's own friend and of course Tilly and according to Susan's investigation's several others still to be proven, to be recompensed. Yes he would have to wait but he would never let *Simon* go to the security of prison, no he had other plans that he owed to his Tilly !!!

The next morning the whole office was buzzing. Oliver arrived fresh as a daisy but Toby looked more like he hadn't slept for a month but it didn't bother anybody, the atmosphere was electric.

Boards went up, pads came out at the ready and the briefing began.

Susan had already arrived and was setting out her findings.

Toby had planned out just who was going to do what and after getting everyone up to date he passed out his plans. These included officers paired and assigned to each attack that Susan had discovered. Neither Toby or Oliver had been down to see *Simon*, he had been left in his cell while they decided just how to go about interviewing him. Whether to tell him all they knew or just begin with the murder of Sam's dad. They knew he was Tyler and *Simon* and thought that maybe the best move would be to get a police phycologist to assess him before they even tried to talk to him. They had no idea of what had gone on in his brain. They just thought that he had changed his name but Susan had suggested that maybe there was some kind of other reason as to his sudden changes of character.

They called Dr Frank Turner and explained they would appreciate his opinion. He happily agreed to come over later that day.

Once he arrived Toby explained about Sam, her dad's murder, Dylan, Tyler's (as he had called himself then) son and the new baby whom he didn't even know if it had survived having left Sam screaming on the floor after he had attacked her.

Dr Frank was intrigued and said he was very interested in the case.

An interview was prepared for Dr Turner to talk to *Simon*. He said he wanted to be alone with him but Toby suggested that a PC could sit in the corner of the room (where the emergency bar is only inches away) but he didn't say that was the reason to the Doctor, just that he thought it might be helpful for somebody else to hear what *Simon* has to say as a totally unbiased and inexperienced opinion.

Dr Turner agreed.

Simon was brought to the room. He hadn't said a word since he was arrested, other that he wanted a drink of water. He had eaten everything they had offered him and had been a model prisoner.

Frank Turner walked in and sat opposite *Simon.*

"Hello, my name is Doctor Turner and I am here to see if you are well enough to be interviewed for several crimes you are suspected of committing. This device, and he pointed to the recorder at the end of the table, is going to record our meeting, do you understand *Simon?* May I call you *Simon* or do you prefer Tyler?"

The model prisoner suddenly woke up, jumped out of his seat as far as the handcuffs that were attached to the side of the table would allow.

"I'm fucking *Simon,* don't ever confuse me with that prat Tyler or you will regret it!"

"OK I'm sorry *Simon* it is then, now please calm down."

Simon relaxed a little and sat back down.

"Now I want to ask you about your family"

"No"

"Yes *Simon*, I need to know. Especially if there is anybody I should tell that you have been arrested. Surely you want somebody to know?"

"No"

"OK lets talk about something else, do you know why you have been arrested?"

"Fuck off!"

"Come on *Simon* this is no way to continue. We can find out all these things but it would be a lot quicker if you talk to me. Is there anybody who might be worried about you? Maybe you have a wife or girlfriend of even your mother or father who are anxious to know your whereabouts?"

"Fuck off!"

After an hour of this one way conversation with the only response of "fuck off!" or "no" Frank Turner stood and switched off the recording machine, folded up his note book and and left the room leaving *Simon* just sitting with a smirk on his face.

Toby and Oliver were watching from the outer office via the video screen. They watched as *Simon* had an extremely harsh reaction to the name

Tyler. They also noticed the smug expression that appeared on his face as soon as the doctor apparently gave up on him.

Frank came into where they were watching. *Simon* was still sitting in the same position and with the same look on his face. The PC was fidgeting in the corner of the room and looked very uncomfortable ....unlike the prisoner.

“Well?” Toby asked “any ideas? Was that a waste of time?” a genuine question and said without any hint of sarcasm.

“Not at all” Frank responded “I'll leave him there to stew for an hour or so, maybe give him a cup of tea but nothing more, then I'll go back in and do it all over again”

It was after lunch before Frank returned to talk to *Simon* who had eaten a huge lunch that he had insisted was his right to have, even though the doctor had advised against it, and was feeling very cocky. Frank could tell by the look on his face and the way he greeted him when he entered the interview room.

“Come to have another “little talk”?” *Simon* said very sarcastically as Frank pulled out the chair opposite him and went to sit down,

“I wouldn't bother to sit down mate” he said “ I'm not saying a word until my brief gets here”

“I'm not here to interview you, Frank started “I am purely here to see if you are in a fit state to be interviewed” with the emphasis on the BE.

Simon just smirked “Well I don't care what you are here for, I'm not saying a word without a brief so you might as well fuck off!”

“OK then” Frank said pulling out the chair and sitting on it anyway. “If you don't want to talk to me that's fine, I'll talk to Tyler instead.”

That hit the spot. *Simon* jumped out of his chair and tried to get at the doctor flaying his arms about but the restraints held fast so he couldn't reach him.

The doc didn't say a word for a full five minutes. *Simon* was shouting and screaming at him to bugger off leaving the doctor unsure as to whether it was aimed at him or at Tyler.

Eventually he calmed down a little and flopped back in his chair, more from exhaustion at flaying his arms and screaming than anything else.

Tyler was beginning to wake up and *Simon* wasn't sure what was going on in his head. He knew it ached and the pain was becoming unbearable. He put his head in his hands and when he looked back up the doctor could see tears in his eyes.

"I'm here" a quiet voice said

Frank thought immediately that he was now talking to Tyler.

"Tell me about yourself" he asked very gently "Do you want me to contact anybody to let them know you are here?"

"My wife" Tyler said "I would love to see my wife, and Dylan of course. I haven't seen them in ages. *Simon* won't let me , he told me they are were dead but I don't believe him. I can give you their address, well actually I was there yesterday I think, but *Simon* dragged me away so I didn't get to see them."

For a moment Toby , Oliver and Susan who were listening and watching in the room a little further down the corridor, felt chills. Did he really know where Sam and the babies were, then relief as Tyler continued.

"We were in Guildford and went to my house, well almost. Then *Simon* drove us away. We had a fight and *Simon* put me back to sleep. That's what he does you know. He can make me sleep anytime he wants to. I don't know how he does it but he does"

Frank almost felt sorry for the poor man in front of him. Yes he had done some terrible things but just how much of them did he actually know had happened. Then of course he realised that he was still talking to *Simon.* Or was he !!!

Suddenly The man put his head down onto the table again and screamed that his head hurt.

Frank decided that enough was enough, this man needed medical treatment before any psychiatric assessments could be done let alone interviews for the horrendous crimes he had supposedly committed. He was a clever man as well as delusional, in the past fifteen minutes had he been talking to a clever *Simon* or a pathetic Tyler. He had assumed Tyler but was *Simon* so clever he could switch so convincingly. Was the headache Tyler breaking though and genuine pain or was it all an act. This case was no easy assignment. He would need a lot more help.

He left the room, with the man still with his head on the table and moaning in pain.

As soon as he walked out of the door Toby was there waiting.

"I have asked for the doctor to come straight away and see him" he told Frank who nodded in agreement.

"Have you any idea just what is going on in his head Doc?" He asked

"Well, he is definitely in no fit state to be interviewed at the moment" Frank said " and as for my opinion well the jury is still out I'm afraid. He is either a very very clever individual or he has two people going on inside his head and I am not sure if he can control either of them. I think I will need to think hard and get some others opinions, I don't think I have ever come across a case quite like this one before."

Just as this conversation was going on they suddenly heard a banging coming from the interview room and the alarm button being pressed. They rushed inside to find the police constable, who had been sitting with

Simon, trying to stop him banging his head on the table. There was blood everywhere which looked like it had come from his nose. The poor constable was helpless in trying to calm him down. Frank jumped into action and held *Simon*'s head from behind while Toby moved the frightened PC out of the way and put his hand under *Simon*'s chin. They couldn't tell whether he was having some type of fit or if he was acting. Luckily the doctor had just arrived and as soon as he saw what was going on he administered a drug to calm him down. It took a few minutes to work but eventually *Simon* just flopped back in the chair and relaxed, leaving Frank still holding his head so as not to let him choke on the blood pouring out of his nose.

“What ever was going on?” the Doctor was asking “How long was he like this for?”

The PC who had been with him explained that *Simon* had just been sitting with his head on the table when suddenly he started to twitch violently and then started banging his head and screaming.

“Well” the doctor said “It does sound like some type of fit but we will know more when we get him to the hospital.”

Toby and Oliver were very worried about letting him out of their sight as they both knew exactly what he was capable of but what choice did they have?

“Can you make sure he is sedated enough not to cause any bother getting him into the ambulance and to the hospital?” Toby asked the doctor

“Have you no sympathy for this poor soul ?” the doctor replied “He looks in quite a bad way and you want me to knock him out with more drugs?”

This was too much for Toby, quietly he took the doctor to one side and whispered “this poor soul as you put it is suspected of murdering several people in cold blood and injuring several others, we have been trying to catch him for years, maybe you will appreciate that I don't want him getting loose and carrying on his murderous ways, so I am sorry if I sound unsympathetic . I also know that he can act superbly well and I am not convinced that he has had a fit, he may well be play acting"

"OK" the doctor said "I can understand your concern but I do believe him to be genuine and we need to get him checked out. I will ensure he is sedated enough not to cause you concern but I am not going to knock him out"

"Of course not doc, I didn't mean that, just enough to allow us to get him to the hospital safely. I will send two police officers in the ambulance with him and I must insist that he is cuffed at all times."

The doctor nodded and nothing more was said.

At the hospital, and once settled into a bed, his face cleaned up and a cuff on his left hand attached to the bed *Simon* was sleeping like a baby. A police constable was sitting on a chair at the end of the room with a news paper and a styrofoam cup of coffee. The door to the room was locked and there were two policemen on chairs just outside.

The doctors at the hospital had been told of the importance of the security and had said they would wait for *Simon* to sleep off the sedative before doing any tests on him. They were in agreement with the police doctor that *Simon* had probably suffered some type of fit and they promised Toby that they would not move him unless there was a police presence.

The two officers outside the room were in contact with the PC inside and before Toby left he checked.

"Sleeping like a baby" the PC inside said.

Toby and Oliver left ensuring that the two officers outside the room knew not to unlock the door unless there was a fire !!!!

Simon was enjoying himself. He had dozed for a little but pretended to be knocked out so the doctor hadn't topped him up with anything more. "Stupid quack" he thought to himself. "How easy it had been to fool him!"

Now his problem was to get the key for his cuffs from the PC , if in fact he had the key. Maybe the ones outside his door had the key. Hmmm he would have to think hard. What could he remember about being cuffed when he was brought into the room, yep got it, the guy in the room had done it so he must have the key. Now to bide his time, let the stupid PC think he was out for the count and drop his guard.

Simon waited until the PC had read his paper, he had walked over to *Simon*, leaned over him, so close that *Simon* could feel his breath on his face. He so wanted to grab him but of course the cuff on his left hand was tight. The PC went back to his chair and reported to the guys outside that "The prisoner is still out of it" he then leaned back in his chair and closed his eyes.

Simon waited until he heard a very gentle snore and the suddenly started to twist and turn and make gurgling noises. The PC jumped up not realising what was going on in his half sleep mode and rushed to *Simon's* side, by which time *Simon* was gasping for air...apparently... and desperately trying to get his left hand up to his face.

The poor PC didn't know quite what to do so he undid the cuff..... that was the biggest mistake he could have made. As soon as has left hand was free *Simon* grabbed the PC and head butted him so hard, breaking his nose and making him fall backwards. As soon as he did this *Simon* put his foot on his neck. It didn't take many seconds with the blood running down his throat and the weight of *Simons* foot on his neck for the poor guy to stop breathing.

Quickly *Simon* swapped clothes with the man and dragged him up into the bed where he covered him with the blanket. He grabbed his shoes from the bedside cabinet where some kind soul had put them when he was brought in. Now how to get the other two in here. He had no doubt that he could deal with them once they were inside but how to get them to unlock the door and come in.

Of course, he had the radio in his pocket that they had been chatting on. OK good reason to call them in, he didn't want to alarm them in case they summoned help.

"Oh *Simon* you are just too clever" he said to himself and switched on the radio.

"Hi"he said into it "can one of you guys come in her for a minute and take over please, I need to pop down to the pharmacy and get my prescription. I totally forgot to get it before we got rushed over here and if I don't have my pills I'll suffer for the rest of the night"

The guys outside looked at each other , they knew they shouldn't open the door.

"Is he sleeping" they one of them asked

"Like a baby" was the reply.

Well what harm can it do they both thought.

As soon as *Simon* heard the key turn he raised the chair he was holding up high above his head, in came one of the policemen, whack, down he went. The other rushed in to see what had happened and whack down he went too, they were obviously not going to stay down but it gave *Simon* just enough time to get out of the door and lock it.

By the time the PCs had got up and raised the alarm *Simon* was at the front of the hospital and heading towards a guy just opening the drivers door of his car.

Simon ran up the the man and told him he would need his car as there was an escaped prisoner getting away and he needed to follow. The man hesitated for a moment while he processed the request, too long for *Simon*, he punched the man in the face, grabbed his keys and jumped into the car and sped away. Within minutes of this happening four police cars, sirens blasting and lights flashing came racing up to the front of the building. Several officers jumped out and ran into the entrance, Toby was nearest to the man who had just been punched and was holding a hanky up to his nose.

"Hey" he said to Toby "one of your men just punched me!"

Toby turned ready to tell the man he was too busy to stop but something made him listen. He motioned Oliver to continue going in with the others while he turned to the man.

"One of our officers punched you?" he asked

"Yeah" the man said " he told me he needed my car to chase a prisoner and then just punched me in the face and drove off in my car!"

Toby immediately shouted for Oliver to come back and bring another officer with him. Then he calmed the man down and took the licence number of his car. Quickly explained to the PC Oliver had brought with him and told him to sort it out while he and Oliver got into their car and headed off in pursuit of the car *Simon* had stolen. While driving Oliver sent out a radio message for all police cars to look out for the stolen vehicle.

The man had said *Simon* looked as if he turned left as he left the hospital and luckily it was a one way so they at least some idea of the direction he had headed.

They had only gone a couple of miles or so before they got a call that the car had been spotted by camera as it was weaving in and out of traffic on the duel carriageway heading out of town towards Haywards Heath.

Toby put on the lights and siren and headed in the same direction.

Suddenly Oliver shouted, "Over there" and pointed to a three car pile up on the junction where the dual carriageway ended. They pulled over just as they saw *Simon* pulling one of the people out of one of the cars that wasn't damaged much and was driving away. Toby left Oliver sorting the crash out and followed behind the new stolen car.

It didn't get too far as it must have sustained more damage than *Simon* thought as the front tyre was almost totally flat. Still he kept driving it although it was pulling strongly to one side. They were in the town now and there were traffic lights ahead so there was nowhere for him to go but into the multi story car park. But with Toby hot on his trail what was he going to do?

“Seems like your luck has run out!” Tyler said as they drove higher and higher .

“Fuck off you stupid prat!” *Simon* shouted back.

“I might be a stupid prat but I know all you can do is give up now!”

“Never!” *Simon* shouted “I'd rather die”

By this time the car was as far as it could go, the top of the car park, eight levels up.

Toby was about 50 metres behind. He jumped out of the car and ran towards *Simon.*

By the time he reached him he had climbed up onto the ledge. With the car park and Toby on one side of him and a sheer drop the other.

Toby stopped in his tracks and stood amazed at the sight before him. The man was arguing with himself but in two different voices.

Toby started to walk very slowly towards him.

“Get back!” *Simon* snarled.

“Come and get him!” another more genteel voice said.

“Fuck off Tyler, you don't know what you are saying!”

“I do, *Simon* it's over, you have to give up!”

The more the argument went on the closer Toby was getting. The adrenalin pumping around Toby's veins was unbelievable. He was almost close enough that if he lurched forward he could possibly push *Simon*. The thought went through his head. Just how many times he had thought of such a moment. How many times he had looked at Tilly in her comatose state and promised her that he would kill *Simon*. Just how many times he had woken in the night planning ways of beating him to death. How often had he prayed for an opportunity to rid the planet of this evil destructive man.

Then Tyler spoke.

"I want you to know that I never wanted to do any of the things *Simon* has done, I want you to know that I loved Sam and Dylan. I want you to know that *Simon* must die so obviously I must die too"

The voice was so sad and so pathetic that Toby almost felt sorry for him. He almost wished he could kill *Simon* but save Tyler but of course that was totally impossible.

Then the evil voice took over.

"You'll never take me you bastard!" it screeched, almost like a banshee.

Toby was frozen to the spot. All the things that had gone through his mind disappeared as his policeman's head took over, as he knew it would when the time came.

"Come on mate, you're not going to jump, let me help you down." He took a tentative step a little closer and stretched out his arm for *Simon* to grab. Just at that moment Oliver and several more police officers arrived.

Oliver looked at Toby, but Toby just shook his head as if to say "It's OK mate, I'm not going to do anything stupid" Oliver understood and nodded back.

And then Oliver very calmly said "Come on *Simon*, there is no way out now, you have to let Toby help you down"

Then everything happened although in a flash it almost seemed like a film put into slow motion.

Oliver moved behind Toby and held on to his other arm, Toby leaned forward to try and grab *Simon*, a sad little voice shouted "Let me go!" and a vicious voice said "NEVER......" then there was silence. !!!!!

A scream from the pavement below said everything.

As the guys all raced down, some on foot some in their cars Toby and Oliver just walked to the ledge and looked over.

"You did the right thing" Oliver said "I knew you would in the end."

"You know me too well Oli" Toby said. "But I had the chance, I feel better knowing I had the chance and didn't take it. I'm bloody glad he did it himself though!"

Epilogue

“Are you sure you have to go back?” Oliver said as he was driving Toby to the air port.

“Of course” Toby said “I have some loose ends to tie up but I'll be back”

“You once said how well I know you” Oliver said “ and I know you will stay in New Zealand, but you are not going to get rid of me that easily. I'm bringing the family over for a few weeks just as soon as you are settled OK?”

“Definitely OK!”

After a quick beer, well beer for Toby and lemonade for Oliver, They gave each other big guy hugs and Toby went through to the departure lounge.

“Don't forget to Zoom as soon as you are sorted or I will get it in the neck from the kids!”

“I won't” and with a tear in his eye, although Oliver didn't see it, Toby turned and walked away.

He had done what he came to do. He would go back to New Zealand, visit Tilly's grave and tell her all about how *Simon* would never hurt anybody again.

Three days after arriving in New Zealand, having had a solid 24 hours sleep at his parents house and a massive fry up breakfast that his mother had insisted he eat before going anywhere, Toby slipped off to visit Tilly's grave.

He bought some beautiful roses, Tilly's favourite flowers, from the florist near the cemetery and headed for her resting place.

When he arrived he was surprised to find several bunches of flowers, although quite dried up, lying on the grave. He gently picked up the shrivelled bunches and put them to one side and the laid his in their place, pulling up a few straggly weeds as he knelt to do so.

As he moved the bunches he noticed there were cards with a couple of them. The writing on them was a little faded but still legible, just. The first one said “It is with great sadness I ask this and I have no right but but do you think you will ever let him go? All my love xx”

The second one said “I had no right to ask you please forgive me. All my love xx”

Toby thought for a moment then dismissed them as he had no idea what or who they were about or to.

He knelt for a while telling Tilly how much he had loved her and how she was safe now but he just wished he had been able to do more while she was still alive. He hoped she would understand if he went on with his life now.

When he had finished he stood and put the dried up flowers in the box left out for such a purpose. Then turned to head away from the grave only to see a figure heading towards him. It was Suzie Tompak. The nurse who had nursed Tilly through her coma and been with her when she died.

Toby was surprised but thrilled to see her.

“Do you come her often?” he said then realised just how it had come out and they both giggled a little. “I mean why are you here ?”

“I come every few weeks” she said “to visit Tilly. I knew you weren't in the country and I felt she needed a friend so I just bring a few flowers and talk to her. I may not have known her when she was err.. well , herself , but I had grown to love her in a way. Does that sound weird ? I don't mean it to”

“Not at all” Toby said “I'm glad you cared enough, I think it is really sweet of you. Do you want to pop those flowers next to mine and then we can walk back together if you like”

Suzie complied and laid the flowers next to his. They started to walk back but after a few steps Toby suddenly said “I've just got to pop back for a second, something I forgot to say, I won't be a second”

As soon as he looked at her flowers he knew. He lifted the card and read the words “Thank you Tilly, if he agrees I promise I will look after him and make him happy”

He knew then where the other cards had come from and just what she was asking her.

They walked back though the cemetery together and as they walked Toby held her hand.

Printed in Great Britain
by Amazon